STORYTELLERS' HAVEN

EDITED BY LYNSEY EVANS

First published in Great Britain in 2024 by:

YoungWriters® —— Est. 1991 ——

Young Writers
Remus House
Coltsfoot Drive
Peterborough
PE2 9BF
Telephone: 01733 890066
Website: www.youngwriters.co.uk

Printed and bound in the UK by BookPrintingUK
Website: www.bookprintinguk.com
YB0586P

FOREWORD

For our latest competition, The Glitch, we asked secondary school students to turn the ordinary into the extraordinary by imagining an anomaly, something suddenly changing in the world, and writing a story about the consequences. Whether it's a cataclysmic twist of fate that affects the whole of humanity, or a personal change that affects just one life, the authors in this anthology have taken this idea and run with it, writing stories to entertain and inspire. We gave them an added challenge of writing it as a mini saga which forces them to really consider word choice and plot. We find constrained writing to be a fantastic tool for getting straight to the heart of a story.

The result is a thrilling and absorbing collection of tales written in a variety of styles, and it's a testament to the creativity of these young authors, and shows us just a fraction of what they are capable of.

Here at Young Writers it's our aim to inspire the next generation and instil in them a love of creative writing, and what better way than to see their work in print? The imagination and skill within these pages show that we might just be achieving that aim! Congratulations to each of these fantastic authors, they should be very proud of themselves.

CONTENTS

Emma Weeramunda (12)	69
Gethin Hardy (12)	70
Mowada Sulaman (12)	71
Charlotte Jones (11)	72
Kitan Sanya (12)	73
Rose Brown (11)	74
Mia Navin (14)	75
Thomas Gill (11)	76
Anabel Gerrard (12)	77
Bryony-Jade Donnelly (11)	78
Johnathon Wade-lavell (13)	79
Daisy Nother (12)	80
Harry Tolson (11)	81
Annie Gittins (13)	82
Ehsan Nadim (11)	83
Beth Telford (11)	84
Lily Dixon (12)	85
Annabel Senior (13)	86
Macy Grayson (13)	87
Charlotte Hardiman (12)	88
Reis Barnsley (11)	89
William Tebbutt (11)	90
Mason Padgett (11)	91
Hayden Bushby (11)	92

Ormiston Forge Academy, Cradley Heath

Evie Ralph (14)	93
Scarlett Reece (12)	94
Yusuf Tekdal (12)	95
Clarissa Ward (11)	96
Poppy Rydes (11)	97
Kyrah-Louise Leighton (12)	98
Syeda Fatima (12)	99
Sidrah Marwa (11)	100
Jasmeet Singh (11)	101
Fatima Ateeq (12)	102
Harriet Brazier-Adams (11)	103
Amelie Starns (11)	104
Lara Bowater-Jones (12)	105
Aleena Zeeshan (12)	106
Oliver Earp (12)	107
Lilly Priest (12)	108

Mac Sefton (11)	109
Summer Woods (12)	110
Archie Bosworth (11)	111
Summer Vanes (15)	112
Dawood Younis	113
Keeley Jade Drake (12)	114
Amal Ghaleb (11)	115
Perry Sheldon (11)	116
Jayden Such (12)	117
Alexa Marshall (11)	118
Liam Darby (13)	119
Ruby Kite (11)	120

Sacred Heart Grammar School, Newry

Kate O'Mahony (11)	121
Kate Toner (11)	122
Isabella Healy (12)	123
Megan Bottell (11)	124
Lauren Cumiskey (12)	125
Cara Cunningham (12)	126
Liadán Farrell (13)	127
Ellen McGivern (12)	128
Laura Syrokosz (12)	129
Sinead McAllister (11)	130
Carragh McShane (12)	131
Lucy Doran (11)	132
Aoife Hayes (11)	133
Molly Keenan (11)	134
Aine McQuaid (12)	135
Orlaith McCoy (12)	136
Nora McCusker (12)	137
Genevieve Lennon (11)	138
Amy Harper (11)	139
Evelyn Joan Kennedy (11)	140
Hannah Begley (12)	141
Sarah McAleenan (12)	142
Niamh McShane (12)	143
Orlaith Rice (12)	144
Ruth-Alice McKinney (11)	145
Isobel Mackin (12)	146
Ellie Mooney (11)	147
Ava Cowan (12)	148

Emma Stevenson (12)	149
Eve Burke (11)	150
Megan Murphy (11)	151
Stella Padden (11)	152
Sophie McGeeney (11)	153
Lucy Gribben (11)	154
Aoibhin Mulligan (12)	155
Cara O'Hare (13)	156
Lena Wojciechowska (12)	157
Eve Convery (12)	158
Amy McLorinan (12)	159
Chloe O'Hare (12)	160
Fion McCrink (11)	161
Cara Magill (11)	162
Megan Galbraith (12)	163
Kara Leckey (12)	164
Erin McCrink (11)	165
Charlotte McGreevy (11)	166
Mary O'Loughlin (11)	167
Ella Keenan (12)	168
Melissa Moley (12)	169
Grace Donnelly (12)	170
Aoibheann McMahon (13)	171
Ava McIntyre (11)	172
Bella McCoy (12)	173
Sarah Main (12)	174
Iga Malcher (12)	175
Elana Sheppard (12)	176
Molly Coulter (12)	177
Cara McAteer (12)	178
Anna McCusker (11)	179
Sienna McAllister (12)	180
Lucy McGrath (12)	181
Caitlin Morgan (11)	182
Sophie Hughes (11)	183
Emma Lowery (11)	184
Yasmin Frizell (11)	185
Heidi Small (12)	186
Mēabh McAleavey (12)	187

Tabor Academy, Braintree

Imogen Webb (11)	188
Annie-Mae Dunlop (11)	189
Tyler Webb (12)	190
Tiegan Rudd (16)	191
Theo Warner (12)	192
Logan Taylor (11)	193
AJ Cooper (13)	194
Hayden Stocker	195

Wycliffe Prep School, Stonehouse

Ellie Mouselli (12)	196
Liam Etheridge (12)	197
William Hewson (13)	198
Sam Smalley (12)	199
Isabella Watt (13)	200
Kitty Ashbee (13)	201
Charlie Geddes (13)	202
Jessica Chambers (13)	203
Isla-Sian Egan (13)	204
Jacob Ockwell (12)	205

THE
STORIES

UNTITLED

"You're early," said Death. "What happened?"

"I'm not dead. I've just gone to sleep haven't I?" said Jake.

"Oh no," he began.

"Nightmares are becoming my reality."

Death exclaimed, "No, you are dead."

"Was my Death planned?" said Jake.

Death went silent.

"Hello, are you there?" said Jake. "This isn't possible, not knowing where I am, only one thing coming to mind. Am I in a simulation?"

Three hearts popped up above Jake. Jake began to play, thinking it was the only way out.

Suddenly, one heart left, but Jake jumped too short and *bam!* Jake was gone.

Rose Hartley (12)
Kettlethorpe High School, Wakefield

THE GLITCH

It was a typical Tuesday afternoon and twelve-year-old Grace had just got home and was rushing to see her two favourite people.

"Dad, Pippa. I'm home!" she yelled.

"We're in here," he exclaimed.

"*Woof!*" barked Pippa.

Excitedly, she opened the ancient door. *Zoom. Bang.* "Ouch." Blackness.

All Grace saw for a few hours was black until she woke up. Cautiously, she stood up but she felt different and light-headed. She saw Pippa.

"Hi, Grace. I'm hungry," Pippa grumbled.

"Argh!" Grace bellowed.

There must have been a glitch in her dad's machine. What had he done?

Francesca Hamby (13)
Kettlethorpe High School, Wakefield

A DEATHLY MEETING

"You're early," says Death. "What happened?"
I walk around the empty darkness. I look deep into the black orbs staring at me. She has a long black coat. Her face is a sheet, apart from two black spheres that seem to be looking deep into my soul.
"Who are you?" I say curiously.
"I am Death," the figure replies.
"What do you mean 'early'?" I say, hoping it's not what I think it is.
"I'm going to guess you don't know."
I give her a look of confusion.
"What?" I reply, longing for an answer.
She looks down.
"You're dead!"

Emily Craig (13)
Kettlethorpe High School, Wakefield

THE HAND OF A PAINTING

Ravi stroked the rough brush, splatting indigo glam all over the page. The half-made astronaut waved and pulled his hand out. Smiling, the painting flickered slightly. Ravi plastered a fake smile and hesitated. His imaginary writings floated around the room, his autistic mind controlling their position. Autistic he is, can't help it. For the sake of his painting's feelings, reaches in. Ravi opens his eyes. A black figure with a worried look, staring at him. "You're early..." said Death. "What happened?"
"Please take me," Ravi said scared. Finally, Ravi was now free, in his own happy and excited world!

Maryam Adnan (11)
Kettlethorpe High School, Wakefield

THE MYTHICAL BEAST

We buried it, but it was back for revenge. Screaming swirled at all angles. Fire crackled and flickered as everyone panicked. "Akira," a voice echoed. Dragons soared through the sky, their roars louder than a lion. They ranged from bright golds to silvery whites, ocean blues to fiery reds and oranges. "Akira!" the familiar voice boomed once more. She blinked. Her friend, Sam, was waving her hand in front of Akira's face.

"Sorry," Akira nervously said. The smell of sweat overwhelmed her senses, dripping down her back and her forehead. Slowly, she looked around, petrified. This is only the beginning...

Alexis Whiteley (12)
Kettlethorpe High School, Wakefield

GRAVITY DISAPPEARS

On a frosty morning, I was sitting in my English classroom at second period. I peered out the window. The rain. The rain wasn't going down, but up!
Suddenly, the building jolted and drifted upwards. All the children were shoved into the ceiling.
Screams. Terrifying, haunting screams. They filled the whole school and my head.
"Grab each other's hands," screeched the teacher.
As I felt the sweating palms against my face, I knew this was the end. We all did. Then I heard a cold, skin-crawling voice.
"You're early," said Death.
Confused, scared, I felt my heart skip a beat...

Silke Schwoch (12)
Kettlethorpe High School, Wakefield

THE GLITCH

Excitement filled the air. They had done it, launched a satellite that connected the world. The celebration was short-lived. A virus had appeared and was corrupting the hard drive! Attempting to stop it, keyboards began clacking, but it was hopeless. The damage had been done! Our supervisor came flying into the room, filled with rage. *Blam, blam, blam!* Three engineers, dead. *Blam, blam, blam!* Three more. He was on a ferocious rampage and nothing could stop him. There was nothing to do but wait for him to run out of bullets. *Blam!* The computerised world moving around me turned a deep black...

Jacob Medina (11)
Kettlethorpe High School, Wakefield

RETURN OF THE BOOK

We buried it but it was back.

Walking to the front door, I felt a sense of sickness and dizziness. But then I stumbled upon something... a book.

"What's what?" Riley shouted.

"I have no clue," I replied.

I kicked the book away from me, completely ignoring what had happened.

I went inside.

"I'm bored. There's nothing to do here," I mumbled.

A loud thump bellowed through my ears.

Curiously, I walked into the other room and there it was, that book again. What was that doing here again? The book slammed against the table and opened on its own...

Ava Halstead (13)
Kettlethorpe High School, Wakefield

THE CLOCKS AND THE RABBIT

Suddenly, the clocks stopped. When it happened I thought I was in danger until I remembered a signal from earlier.
All the clocks started flickering.
I heard a random voice behind me saying, "You can fix it, find him."
I was really confused.
My rabbit, sitting next to me, said, "It's me, I'm speaking."
I jumped back in fear.
I thought it was just a mysterious dream, but then my mum and sister came running up the stairs.
Suddenly the clocks started again and my rabbit disappeared! I got confused about why the clocks stopped and why my rabbit was talking.

Niamh Barnes (11)
Kettlethorpe High School, Wakefield

NO ESCAPE

She ran along the halls of the building. The carpets tripped her up and the books were flying everywhere. Her blonde hair getting in the way of her eyesight. "Help!" Suddenly, she ran into a room that she hadn't seen before. Number one. *This hotel is strange*, she thought. Panicking, Sofie shut the door behind her, forgetting to scan the room first.
"You're early," said Death. "What happened?" boomed a menacing voice.
Sofie stared at the wall. She felt as though it was telling her to give up and that is what she did. "I can't let me be taken..."

Beth Buckley (11)
Kettlethorpe High School, Wakefield

A GLITCH IN REALITY

Jim was making his lunch, a cheese and ham sandwich and a cheese and onion sandwich for his younger brother. Suddenly, everything went black. As he trembled in his boots, he appeared to stand in an eerie black room filled with voices saying their last words - "Help me! Set me free!" His eyes darted across the room. He was being approached by a dark silhouette. Who was it? What was happening? A million things were rushing around in his head, a million possibilities.

Closer and closer and closer - footsteps echoed throughout the dark mysterious room. Were they angry? Did they want to kill?

Joel Stokoe (11)
Kettlethorpe High School, Wakefield

THE GLITCH

"You're early," said Death. "What happened?"

Early one winter cold morning, I was strolling through the park, my long, soft, blonde hair blowing through the bitter wind. In the flash of an eye, I was being dragged into the back of a car. *Boom!*

Now I'm here. It doesn't look like I belong here, though. Flaming hot fire and echoing screams howl through the burning air.

"Is this what Hell is really like?"

On my way to find the head to remeasure my sins and good deeds, I see some horrifying sights. Finally, I'm here in the place I belong.

Molly Walsh (13)
Kettlethorpe High School, Wakefield

OH DEAR EMMA

Every clock had stopped. Emma began rummaging through more of her father's documents. *Me, an alien?* she thought. Unfortunately, she could not handle it and burst into tears. Shockingly some weird green goo came out of her tears and she transformed into a psycho alien. She ran downstairs. Her 'father' saw her. "Sweetheart, it's okay! Come with me!" he said in a polite, caring tone. She decided to follow him. After some time, they reached his lab and she sat down. Suddenly the lights turned off. Out of nowhere a sound of a gunshot was heard. Everything had finally ended.

Maryum Ali (12)
Kettlethorpe High School, Wakefield

UNTITLED

"You're early," said Death.

"Sorry, sir."

"It's okay," said Death. "Let's get started. Here is the cloak and the scythe. Now get this person... Well done. You are the new reaper."

But then, ever since he got the job, he had been killing people for no reason. One day, he went way too far and killed his master, the Grim Reaper. The whole world became immortal. No one could die anymore. As time went on, people were getting scared that it would never be a mortal world where they could die peacefully. Would they have to do something...?

Jed Gittins (12)
Kettlethorpe High School, Wakefield

NARHALLA

I woke up, not in my bedroom. Without hesitation, I shot up. Computers, desks, buttons, drawers. I didn't know where I was but I knew I had to leave fast.

I felt abandoned, my surroundings looked abandoned. Not a single light on. As I looked to my right, there was a skull. Not like ours though, something mythical.

Underneath, there was writing stating, "Us of Narhalla!" Who is Narhalla? Where is Narhalla? What is Narhalla? All of a sudden, everything woke up. Every button glowed, and every light shined.

So did a big machine. "You've seen too much!"

Lee H Williamson (12)
Kettlethorpe High School, Wakefield

UNTITLED

Slowly, I scampered out of my bed and woke up in a mysterious, luscious forest filled with pinecones.

Crack.

What was that? I thought to myself, venturing over to where I'd heard it.

Hiding behind a colossal pine tree, I saw a bloodthirsty, ominous creature looking down at me. Standing taller than a skyscraper, the creature picked me up and teleported into a land filled with other creatures.

Luckily, using all my might, I managed to squeeze out of his grip.

"Come over here," whispered a soft voice.

I quickly ran over to the voice...

Sydney Swan (11)
Kettlethorpe High School, Wakefield

LANEY'S NOT SO SWEET SIXTEENTH

What if the world was filled with a 'brilliant vs evil' population? One night, an ordinary girl called Laney sadly met her life-changing dilemma. One night, Laney was bursting with excitement as she was planning her dream Sweet Sixteenth birthday party (which was in a week's time). Although her birthday just sounds like an ordinary birthday, it wasn't. It will be the day that the system will decide if she will be brilliant or evil. She has so much pressure as all her family were selected as brilliant. The day finally came! However, she got selected as evil. What will she do...?

Lottie Fell (11)
Kettlethorpe High School, Wakefield

THE DAY EVERYTHING CHANGED

Surrounding me was vast skyscrapers and crowds of people. Everything was normal that afternoon in NYC. Suddenly, all of the lights cut out leaving the streets in complete darkness. The internet wasn't working and people were terrified. There it was, a huge screen turned on. It was an alert, saying: *'Everyone take cover there is going to be a blast'*. Immediately people got into cars and crowds of people hurriedly ran inside. Suddenly people tried to drive away, but they couldn't, the engines wouldn't start. They were trapped, what could I do? Everyone was hopeless.

Tilly McCann (11)
Kettlethorpe High School, Wakefield

THE GLITCH IN THE SEA

Just two girls on a boat. Everything was normal. The sea was quite calm that day. Until they could see something in the distance. Something dark. Something horrific. A sight they had never seen before. Lily asked her best friend if they should turn back. Maisie was determined to keep going. They slowly got closer realising it was a portal. They soon reached it. The boat elegantly swam through the portal. It was a totally different dimension. They were travelling through their past. Seeing their younger selves talking to each other and having fun. Looking back at their memories from life.

Millie Martin (13)
Kettlethorpe High School, Wakefield

THE DAY OF EVIL

Every clock had stopped. I didn't move but my reflection did.
Suddenly, I was travelling through time but there was a
malfunction, this was an impossible reality.
"You're early," said Death. "What happened?"
"Well, I was just doing my job then somehow an injection
made people act crazy and I got stabbed," I said.
Somehow, I woke up and felt the pain in my back.
"They did not manage to kill you. The whole world is now full
of them, and I'm one of them," something said as I suddenly
woke up.
The world went blank.

Alfie Dorling (12)
Kettlethorpe High School, Wakefield

ALONE

Marcus rose from his bed and opened the curtains to let some light in.
"What a nice day-"
He was soon to realise it wasn't. The world had become a barren wasteland. The sky had turned as dark as outer space and the worst part was that demonic, heartless creatures roamed the lifeless land. He had to make the right choice. He needed to get out there. Who knew... maybe there could still be some people left! Marcus immediately ran down the stairs of his house and opened the front door.
"Yes! There's someone there!"
But it was just a cutout...

Kai Thompson (11)
Kettlethorpe High School, Wakefield

VANISH

Oscar woke up. He then exclaimed, "I just had the worst nightmare! The world had gone."

Later that day he and his cousin, Joseph, went outside, only to realise the sky was glitching. "Oh no!" Both ran downstairs into the basement, hiding from the chaos that had opened up.

Hours passed and so they finally went out again, only to see the world decomposing in front of them. They slowly began to fall into an endless void, and in due course, disappeared too.

Oscar woke up. "I just had the worst nightmare. The world had gone! Wait, oh no! Help!"

Henry Smith (12)
Kettlethorpe High School, Wakefield

I MET DEATH

"You're early," said Death. "What happened?"

I was in shock. I couldn't be dead, could I? I'd only just gone to sleep.

"I-I-I don't know," I stammered.

It was so peculiar. It was a quick nap, not the end of my life. I never would have thought of it like that. Why? How? Who? Questions were running through my head.

Was I poisoned? Was it my time? If I had been murdered I was stumped. I didn't have any enemies. Or was that just what I thought?

All I wanted to know was what had happened to me. Who had done this?

Mollie Richardson (11)
Kettlethorpe High School, Wakefield

UNTITLED

What happened? How did she get there? Where was she? She had only had a short nap. Who was that? Surrounding her were walls of black, and there was a rickety feeling under her. Her hands were tied up in some thick rope. "Oi!" called a croaky voice from the front.

What on earth was happening? She started to cry, but no tears fell from her tear ducts. She started to hyperventilate, yet was screaming inside. Suddenly - *whip!* A large rope strangled her from behind. Everything went black. She gasped-

Little old Charlotte had been asleep the whole time.

Tiana Khall (11)
Kettlethorpe High School, Wakefield

THE ALTERNATE UNIVERSE

"Wait, what?" I look around my room... but it's not my room. *Where am I? What happened?* I think to myself as I get up to look around the rest of my house. But it's no different. I find my mam and ask her to take a look.
"What's up with it?"
"What do you mean 'what's wrong with it?' Have you seen it?"
"It's two in the morning, Jack. Get back to bed!"
I stare at my ceiling when, suddenly, a strange-looking creature jumps down on top of me. The next thing I know is I'm blacked out...

Kendal Johnstone (11)
Kettlethorpe High School, Wakefield

UNTITLED

Tonight me and my best friend, Lottie, are having our first-ever sleepover that we've talked about for ages. As I arrived, I saw her waiting for me, peeking out of the window.
We did lots of fun activities together. We went on her trampoline, built a den, baked together. But then, all of a sudden, the night changed from amazing to terrible in less than five minutes.
My friend started acting weird. She stopped talking in the middle of her sentence and walked to the window, stared at the ground and repeatedly said her dead dog's name. *Bruce, Bruce, Bruce.*

Charlotte Hargrave (14)
Kettlethorpe High School, Wakefield

THE SHINING SAVIOUR

I looked out to the burgundy aqua sunset, the flames surrounding me. I wondered when the people in the silver suits would come and imprison me again. Every night it happened. It used to be only once every fortnight. It wasn't their fault. The moon suddenly disappeared. Our shining saviour had just been demolished from our grasp. I snapped back to reality when I heard the metallic screeching of the machines. Then, the heaving stomping of the figures. I could see their shady silhouettes moving from the horizon, when I realised they were too late. The creatures had already come.

Angelica Bradbrook (11)
Kettlethorpe High School, Wakefield

THE GLITCH

One late night, Harry was on the couch dozing off to sleep while watching TV. A little while later, he heard something, he never wanted to hear.

"Breaking news. 19-year-old William Albans has died on impact."

"What?!" Harry screamed. He couldn't believe what he was hearing.

The next day, it was William's funeral. Harry wandered into the church devastated but what he was about to see would shock him dearly. William at his own funeral and a big dark flare behind him, a sort of smoke. William seemed normal apart from his skeleton hand!

Jack Watson (13)
Kettlethorpe High School, Wakefield

THE STRANGE LIQUID

She was walking towards the place she buried her time capsule seven years ago. When she uncovered the box from underground and opened it, a purple liquid oozed out and she felt faint all of a sudden. She ran to tell her mum. All she said was, "It's back!"
She called the police to tell them they needed to send a notice out to everyone. People ran to underground bunkers, grabbing what they could on the way. We were safe. Her mum told her that this could be the end. The purple liquid started coming underground. "It's over," everyone screamed.

Charlotte Strutt (11)
Kettlethorpe High School, Wakefield

THE OUTSIDER

It's been three months since life was the same, since brushing my teeth was normal, as it should be. It all started when I didn't move but my reflection did. Time seemed to move faster some days, slower other days. There were times it would completely stop.

Last night, I had a flashback of a completely different reality, of something I didn't recall. Whatever it was, it could speak, it told me I was special. I was the only person to notice the peculiar errors that were happening to our reality. This malfunction existing among us called himself the Glitch.

Frankie McKelvie (13)
Kettlethorpe High School, Wakefield

THE GLITCH - STORYTELLERS' HAVEN

THE LOOPED END

It was 3:15, the last five minutes of school. It was Friday.
There was a girl called Raya with short brown hair, emerald-
green eyes, and a boring school uniform. Suddenly, the clock
struck, but no one was in the classroom. She was back at
the door of the class. She ran towards the exit of the school,
but she kept ending up back at the door. No matter what
she did, she was at the door. It had felt like an hour until
everything went cold and dark.
"You're early," said Death. "What happened to you?"
"I don't know," Raya said.

Lexi Johnson (12)
Kettlethorpe High School, Wakefield

THE GLITCH

I rummaged through the remnants of a paper bag. I believed that the fortune of Tokyo, that I had been granted, was caused by my precious collar. It had 'Nigel' displayed in a traditional font and was encrusted with a variety of gemstones. Exceeding my expectations, a tray of sushi appeared from a crumpled newspaper. My spirits and mental state had replenished. Time to explore. Approaching a shadowy forest, an immense rod slit an infinite hole in the ground. Getting closer, I descended into a spectrum of an area of colour. Was this the collapse of the universe?

Violet Jackson (12)
Kettlethorpe High School, Wakefield

THE IMPERSONATION

"You're early," said Death. "What happened?"
I stood up. My head killed. "What?" I murmured. "Where am I?" I looked around, soft, white clouds danced underneath me. I paused as the angel-like figured filled me in. I was dead! Me, dead! According to the replay of my life, my twin sister catfished me into going on a date with her and then she stabbed me to death. I was sent to look over her. She stole my identity and not a single soul noticed, not even my mother. How infuriating. I don't think I could ever get over this.

Maisie Gill (13)
Kettlethorpe High School, Wakefield

THE ANGEL OF DEATH

"You're early," said Death.

I replied, "Am I?"

I was riding my bike so fast that I felt like life paused for a second and then everything slowly started disappearing. I didn't know what was happening, I couldn't believe this was reality, I thought I was in a dream but no! I was not dreaming at all. I thought I had started flying but no! I hadn't. I could now see my guardian angel fading away. I said to myself, "This is the end." Then in a blink of an eye, everything went pitch black and now I'm with Death.

Hamza Bilal (13)
Kettlethorpe High School, Wakefield

THE GLITCH

Here in this dimension, the world has dangerously evolved. My alarm clock goes off and I wake up to a buzzing noise. My robot is making my breakfast. Yes, there are robots! It's the year 2055 and the planet has changed a lot. I have two roommates, Harvey and Joe. Harvey had gone out for an interview for a new job and Joe was in his room playing video games.

I hate how robots have taken over everything. Humans have no more freedom with these around! I highly doubt Harvey will get the job. Everything is powered by robots.

"God, help!"

Faith Harakuta (14)

Kettlethorpe High School, Wakefield

UNTITLED

Imagine you were part alien with four legs and seven arms. Anisha lived on a random planet nobody knew of. Ten weeks ago, Anisha warped down to Planet Earth. She landed in Australia. Walking around, people were glaring at her. *Bang!* The police found her and asked her what she was. She didn't reply because she was a horrific, colossal creature. They stopped Anisha again, got three pairs of handcuffs out and arrested her. Shaking, Anisha got put in cell number 26813 with a creepy old man. He had a secret gun. Anisha hid under the bed and he fired...

Leah Gee (12)
Kettlethorpe High School, Wakefield

THE SUN THAT DIDN'T SET

Angelica and Kye were peacefully sitting by their tree, watching the sunset, while eating chocolate raisins. This peace could never last forever. They came to realise the sun wasn't setting; it was still. In shock and horror, they jumped from their seats. They were moving faster than anything, which meant electricity or anything else wouldn't work. Soon enough, one of them will make the other live with guilt over the other's death, but it does not have to be like this. Why did it have to be her? Why, out of the two of them, was it Angelica?

Izzy Martin (12)
Kettlethorpe High School, Wakefield

THE GLITCH

"Mondays are the worst," I groaned.

We sat playing on our phones. An advert popped up showing an app that claimed to take people back to reality. We saw warnings that this game had changed people. We liked to take risks so, ignoring the warnings, we downloaded the app. Suddenly, it felt like I was travelling through time. We emerged in a world that felt unreal. You could create a world any way you wanted.

"Where are we?" I asked.

A man walking past said, "I can tell you're not from here. Welcome to reality."

Ellissa Crook (13)
Kettlethorpe High School, Wakefield

UNTITLED

It was a normal day when I went to school...

A few hours later, after school, I was talking to my friend when suddenly, a car crashed into me and my friend. Holly, my friend, woke up and started to shake me to wake me up. Holly couldn't wake me up, and she walked away.

I woke up, gasping for air, when I heard someone say, "You're early." It was Death, then he asked, "What happened?"

I had no words. I was still terrified. He sighed.

"I understand you are in shock, but answer me. I need to know."

Jayme Hunt (12)
Kettlethorpe High School, Wakefield

UNTITLED

Every clock had stopped in the castle. "I wonder what is happening," said the boy. The brick started falling down. His dad and Jackson fell down. Dad died and Jackson got a broken leg because he landed on a bed. Jackson went to the hospital by getting on the bus and had surgery but the doctor turned into a robot after his surgery and then he looked out the window and saw a plane saying, 'You are dead' and then it crashed and killed everyone in the hospital. But Jackson survived it and went to the shop and then went to Grandad's.

George Keenan (12)
Kettlethorpe High School, Wakefield

THE GLITCH

As I woke from the nightmare-filled sleep I had endured, everything seemed somewhat normal... until I stepped outside. The landscape started to malfunction and deform wildly as holes began appearing in the sky and ground. After the glitching receded, I found that the ground had caved in from underneath me and I rapidly began to fall into the black abyss as the ground resealed itself, trapping me inside. After hours of falling, I found myself inside of a ruby-red river. After crawling out, I found myself in an alternate reality, an opposite reality...

Bobby Holdsworth (11)
Kettlethorpe High School, Wakefield

THE UNKNOWN UNIVERSE

One day, Jamal woke up to an ordinary day in the state of Kentucky.
He decided to go to work, but suddenly the weather went bad so he went home and took a long nap.
Once Jamal had woken up, he started to travel through time.
Looking around at his surroundings he started to realise that he was stranded in a different universe. He tried to call for help but there was no one around to help him.
Suddenly, a strange noise came from behind him. As he looked around a group of aliens had surrounded him.
"Help!" he cried.

Dior Sofi (11)
Kettlethorpe High School, Wakefield

THE GLITCH - STORYTELLERS' HAVEN

UNTITLED

I'd always wondered what it would be like to be a superhero. Today was the day I found out.
"Lunch is ready."
I took off my headphones and ran downstairs to eat lunch.
After I had eaten my sandwich, I decided to go out to the art shop. When I finally got there, I was looking at the spray paint and felt a little tingle in my hand.
Oh, it was just a spider.
After paying for my spray paint cans, I got home, ate tea (fajitas) and went to bed.
On Sunday, the next morning, around 9am, I woke up as Spider-Man.

Ava Harbinson (12)
Kettlethorpe High School, Wakefield

THE STRANGE

On a boring old school day, a girl called Emma was in her maths class.

It was her last period and as she looked across the classroom, she saw a mythical fire-breathing dragon outside.

As it headed for the classroom, it disappeared. Everyone in her class was stunned as the unbelievable just happened. But as the teacher walked back into the classroom, all of the students tried to get the teacher's attention. Then she shouted back saying they were making her mad.

She tried to calm the class down but the class was too excited.

Elyssia Mawtus-Cardwell (12)
Kettlethorpe High School, Wakefield

WORLD POLLUTION

Hi, I am Ike, telling you about the world's pollution. The environment is changing which is very bad. People are very poor that they can't even poop in the toilet. The world should help one another.

Now cutting down trees and creating more AI or technology that is really bad and evil. But it is not too late. We can stop this pollution by planting more trees and putting more bins on the road, using the technology we have now.

Some places are very poor. We should help them, and we might stop this pollution. Save the world forever.

Ikechukwu James (11)
Kettlethorpe High School, Wakefield

GAME OF LIFE

Every clock had stopped. I lay in bed playing my game as the world glitched before me. This was the end of the world. The game of life had begun. Loud screams of terror came from neighbouring houses as their children were nowhere to be seen. There I stood. I was inside somewhere as a loud voice shouted, "Level one!" The game had started. It began. Humans paced around, moving everywhere, trying to find a way to escape. But it was no use; soon enough, they walked back to the starting point. The end was near and, soon enough, we were home.

Ayo Osisanya (11)
Kettlethorpe High School, Wakefield

THE GLITCH - STORYTELLERS' HAVEN

UNTITLED

Monday, period four, maths. Dan and Tom were about to fall asleep but just then Dan remembered yesterday. He found this strange mysterious clock.
It said, "Click here to stop time. Tap twice with someone. Tap again to unfreeze."
Dan and Tom both tapped it. Just then Dan and Tom dropped it. Tom and Dan didn't care. They went to every sweet store and shared the sweeties. They stole all the money from the bank and drew graffiti all over their horrible school. They started to feel very bad, but there was no going back.

Jack Robins (11)
Kettlethorpe High School, Wakefield

LAST PERSON ALIVE

Ignoring the warnings, I downloaded the app, oblivious to the ongoing hellish destruction just outside my window. Someone knocks on my door. Opening it, my eyes fall upon my friend Lilian, shaking in a little ball. Picking her up, I notice people running for their lives, running from toxic gases that are growing closer by the second. Lilian tells me that we are the last ones alive, before passing out in my arms. I do the only thing I can think of. I slap her. She remains still. I drop her and begin to feel queasy, and then... I collapse.

Lucy Sennett (11)
Kettlethorpe High School, Wakefield

THE APP

It was the summer of 2010 when Kacy was with her friends. She got dared to download an app that tells you how you die. Kacy downloaded it and it showed a picture of her going insane.

She didn't believe this nonsense and laughed it off. About a week later, Kacy noticed weird things. She was filled with anxiety and fear. She tried to delete the app.

"Action failed!" She tried again. "Action failed!" This was horrifying to her. She couldn't bear it anymore. She went to the kitchen and found a knife...

Kaiya Nicholls (11)
Kettlethorpe High School, Wakefield

THE GLITCH

Mia was in her bedroom getting ready for her 18th birthday. She looked into the mirror and saw a movement she didn't make. She stood as still as she ever has and stared. She was there until it stared back and smiled like a psychopath.
Mia screamed as the reflection grabbed her by the neck and pulled her through the mirror into a world she hadn't seen before. Hundreds of people she thought she knew were trapped in small cages.
She turned back as she saw the same figure push her off a cliff and dive through the mirror.

Cara Jefferson (13)
Kettlethorpe High School, Wakefield

UNTITLED

A small orphan boy with tatty clothes was limping home after being beaten up because he had no parents. Through his teared-up eyes, he saw a bright blue book which was strangely familiar. Little Timmy was reminded of hope when he saw it. As he opened it, on the front cover it said *Warning*. Then he decided to test it out by writing *parents*. As he walked back, for the first time ever with a smile, his friend Lanca saw him. She was speechless, all she could say was, "How?"
Let's just say, it did work.

Noah Bardon (12)
Kettlethorpe High School, Wakefield

THE DAY THE GRIND STOPPED

A father wakes up. His daughter stacking crayon drawings on his bedside table. He thought nothing of this until he opened the airlock door at work. When he looked behind him though, there it was, one of his daughter's drawings. A teddy bear on top of lots of chairs. Still, he thought nothing of it. He sat in his chair, took a pill and tried to go to sleep. But they were there. They were always there. This time they weren't kind enough to let him be. They did something much more gruesome. This was sad. His daughter was waiting.

Jack Budd (12)
Kettlethorpe High School, Wakefield

BACKROOM

On a quiet night, I woke up to the whispers of people around me. Looking around I saw the musty yellow wallpaper...
Equipped with just a flashlight I wandered around the maze, passing through lots of twisted realities. The more reality, the more it boosted me to go further. As I walked through one reality a black figure with its body twisted into knots started screaming. The scream pierced my ear. As I ran a whole new reality appeared, one that looked like a hospital which at the top showed a white door. As I ran I fell and...

Gabryel Shoko (12)
Kettlethorpe High School, Wakefield

LOST!

Ignoring the warnings, Bob downloaded the app.
Bob was playing on computer games when something appeared. It was an advertisement for an app. Warnings came up telling him about the consequences. Bob downloaded the app anyway.
All of a sudden he teleported into a game. The game told him to complete tasks to get out. If he didn't succeed he would be there forever. Bob got nervous. His first task was to build a shelter to sleep in. He began to get to work. After that, he completed all the tasks.
Did he ever escape?

Esme Reed (11)
Kettlethorpe High School, Wakefield

THE SILENT WOODS

"You're early," said Death. "What happened?" Their voice echoed in the woods.

Where was everyone, and why was it just me? What day, week, or even year was it? Every time I took a step, I heard the voice, but who was it?

As I ran, the voice got louder. I desperately needed to find shelter, so I ran, and I finally found a sketchy hut. But the voice followed me to the brown, wooden hut. There were so many spiders. I needed to leave this place very soon, so I left, and I sprinted to leave, and then...

Polly Booth (11)
Kettlethorpe High School, Wakefield

UNTITLED

Most Saturdays, I go to my local and buy food. I entered and it was freezing. Silence all around me. I wasn't safe. The door slammed and metal bars covered all around me. A voice spoke. It sounded like Siri. It proceeded to say, "We have captured all humans and the Earth is ours. We'll make you work for us and follow every command we give you. For now, stay put. Siri." I was so scared. A purple alien crawled towards me. He told me that humans were safe and aliens saved humans from AI. Forever on, we hid together.

James Lockwood (13)
Kettlethorpe High School, Wakefield

THE SECRET ORGANISATION

It was a normal day for Esme, hanging out with friends until they tried to enter a secret organisation. She didn't want to, but her peers persuaded her. They were found, but she was the only one that got caught. Gone, possibly forever and with no help at all.

Days later, Esme struggled to escape, but she wasn't good at puzzles. Suddenly, a large door opened with a loud noise. A tall man stood there with a gun in his hand. *Bang!* Esme fell to the ground with bright red blood flooding out of her wounded chest.

Amber Penny (11)
Kettlethorpe High School, Wakefield

A GLITCH IN SOCIETY

It was late in the afternoon on a stormy day. Fred had never seen such violent weather. He started getting ready to go to sleep. He could hear objects breaking around the house and horses neighing. He went to bed. Suddenly, he woke up to a big bang. He heard his family confused and rushed out of bed. They went outside. They were shocked to see nothing but a UFO. Everything had gone. They went closer and the UFO started shaking. Then he got sucked into the UFO. After a minute, he returned. But it was different. He was a hologram.

Sebastian Drobina (13)
Kettlethorpe High School, Wakefield

THE ZOMBIE APOCALYPSE

It was a cold, wintery morning. Two girls were in the mall, walking. Their names were Summer and Lily; they were best mates and were inseparable.

As they were going into a coffee shop, an alarm went off. It was the loudest alarm they ever heard.

Over the PA it shouted, "The zombie apocalypse has begun."

Startled, Lilly ran like crazy whilst Summer stood calm in her spot.

That's when the zombies came. Summer and Lily ran to safety.

Will it be betrayal or will they use friendship to survive?

Zunaira Hussain (13)
Kettlethorpe High School, Wakefield

THE GLITCH

It's ten years later since I became 18. I now have a wife and kids. I couldn't imagine life without them. My son is 9 years old and he is super intelligent. However, one day, my wife and son went missing for a week. I called the police to look for them. They brought dogs but that didn't help either because there was not a trace. They searched and searched, not to be found. Then they just walked through the door, like nothing happened. I asked them where they were and they looked at me all confused, and then silence.

Piotr Luczynski (14)
Kettlethorpe High School, Wakefield

THE GLITCH

One day, a boy called Harry went to bed. He was in the house with his mum and his dad when he went to bed, but something unthinkable happened.

Harry was watching a movie, and when Harry finished it, the TV opened, and Harry got sucked inside of it.

Harry hoped it was a dream, but it was not. Harry couldn't move because he was fearful. He felt stuck, but he wasn't. When he looked around, he started to scream. Suddenly, people from the dead began to come to him.

"You're early," they said...

Zak Lilley (11)
Kettlethorpe High School, Wakefield

THE GLITCH

Dear Diary,

Today is December the eleventh, 2049. It was a normal day. Everyone got a message saying there was a glitch in the system. Scientists were making a time machine and something went wrong. Dinosaurs were back and no one knew how to fix it. Now everyone is getting killed and it's like the end of the world.

Oh no! What's happening? I'm scared. What is it? Am I next? What am I supposed to do? I need help. The dinosaur is after me. Help, please help me. I'm scared! The dinosaur is getting closer!

Layla Kelk (11)
Kettlethorpe High School, Wakefield

ELECTRODE AND THE MYSTERIOUS DEMANDS

Darkness; every light, building, car, plane, phone stopped. Nothing but chaos and darkness. Then, in the blink of an eye, everything was normal, but not the same. Things were just slightly off. People froze on the spot, staring at the advertisement boards.

The Channel 7 news came on, "Are we rolling? Ladies and gentlemen, we have been given the news that the supervillain, Electrode, has taken control. If you look above, you will know his UFO is directly above us. He said chaos will come, so God help us all!"

Noah Riley (14)
Kettlethorpe High School, Wakefield

HOW ONE CLICK CHANGED THE WORLD

Ignoring the warnings, I downloaded the app. I logged on and began to play the game. A player was hacking at first. I thought little of it, but I didn't realise this wasn't just a player who found a glitch; this was someone who wanted to take over the world and make everyone know his name and play his game. He took over tablets, phones, computers. Every device around the world. He sent the world into panic. No one could contact each other. No one could call for help. Over time, we lost more and more - just us left.

Luca Robinson (11)
Kettlethorpe High School, Wakefield

THE DAY EVERYTHING CHANGED

Ignoring the warnings, I downloaded the app. My life was about to change - forever. It was a normal day and little did I know I was in terrible danger. I checked my phone and an ad popped up: *Get this app for a chance to win £1,000,000* my phone bared. As I downloaded this app several warnings popped up. As I waited for the download to finish, I heard screams. I looked out the window and an alien invasion was happening. Then a boulder fell from the sky and my house crumbled to dust killing me in the process.

Noah Edward-Williams (11)
Kettlethorpe High School, Wakefield

THE GLITCH

Once upon a time, there was a kid called Bob and he was sucked into his laptop. Randomly, at first, he thought it was cool then he started to get worried that he couldn't find anyone else in there except himself. After an hour he thought, "I'm gonna be stuck in here forever aren't I?" He was in the multiverse and didn't know how to get out. "Help, help," he shouted, but no one was in there but him. He tried everything he could, but he was truly stuck in there forever. What could he do?

Archie Warring (11)
Kettlethorpe High School, Wakefield

UNTITLED

It was a beautiful day in Old York. The sun was beaming. A young boy called Mason was casually sitting on the sofa when he looked out of the window and saw the whole town screaming and running. He quickly grabbed his coat and ran out the door to see what was going on. As soon as he got outside, he figured out what was going on. His eyes lit up. "A monster is trying to take over the city. What do I do?" he said. "There's nothing I can do." As the monster approached Mason, his heart started to drop.

Mason Goodair (13)
Kettlethorpe High School, Wakefield

THE DRESS

The anomaly girl was dressed in a ghostly smooth dress. It happened in a store, and it was on 23rd September 1934. She wanders around looking for milk, here and there in the store. She finds out that the place where you get the milk is gone, and tries to find out where it was. The ghostly smooth dress turns into the girl, and the girl turns into the dress. Now, since things changed, the ghost could find the milk, but how? Because the ghost was in the girl's body for a while the ghost now feels free and is now happy.

Enhle Ncube (12)
Kettlethorpe High School, Wakefield

THE END OF THE WORLD

Ignoring all the warnings, I downloaded the app not thinking what I could do to the world. As I played, I thought to myself, *what would it be like to be here in this multiverse?* Feeling a bit famished, I went downstairs and that was when I realised I had shut down the world! But that's when I saw The Portal. I never thought it existed, so I entered the realm. Trying and trying multiple times to save what I had done, I gave up. But I realised I could do this. I am going to do this and save the entire world!

Emma Weeramunda (12)
Kettlethorpe High School, Wakefield

FORGETFUL MEMORIES

Hello, I'm Sam. I don't know how to say this, but I think I made everyone forget everything! I love video games and this is one app that kept popping up. I, being a brainless 13-year-old, downloaded it. It had some weird foreign name, but who was I to care?

It showed me a 3D image of the world. I clicked my area and a loud buzzing noise came from upstairs. I ran as fast as I could upstairs. My parents were lying on the floor. They stood up and they let out a *screech!*

They just stood there...

Gethin Hardy (12)
Kettlethorpe High School, Wakefield

THE GLITCH TWITCH

One morning, whilst the rain was pouring, I saw a weird portal which looked very immortal. Suddenly it pulled me in, and the last thing I saw was my fish's fin. I was now in a magical world where my voice could never be heard. I had a migraine from all this mess and all I could think about was how all this made sense. All I could see was everything glitching. It was glitching so much that my eyes started twitching. I saw a figure whose name was The Glitch. He was a figure that was just a twitch, he was petrifying.

Mowada Sulaman (12)
Kettlethorpe High School, Wakefield

THE END

A bony finger slowly pricks my shoulder, with cold breath blowing on my neck. Mist blocks my view, swallowing me into eternal darkness. I whip around gasping for air as terror hurtles around me. I come face to face with something. A shadowy figure draped in all black. Then it hits me... Death! I stumble over, my life flashing before my eyes. He has something in his hand, and he drops it. It pierces through my leg, too sharp to feel it slice deep inside me. It is over. My eyes slowly close, the light dims, I feel my...

Charlotte Jones (11)
Kettlethorpe High School, Wakefield

THE GIFT

The world now has no use of technology, food or electricity. Every day people suffer, and every day people think of the world coming to an end. A sudden noise disturbed Lia, it was so loud she had to get up. When she looked in the mirror she saw her mum, who died five years ago, standing in the corner of the room. At that very second she could see kings and queens of the past. Lia thought for a second, *is this a dream? Or is this a gift of seeing families and ancestors of the past?* Lia could just imagine it.

Kitan Sanya (12)
Kettlethorpe High School, Wakefield

NOT MY LIFE

Charlotte is an ordinary girl and does what every ordinary girl would do after a long day at school - go up to her bedroom and lay on her phone.

But one day when she came home, nobody was there, so she went on a walk around her street, trying to find her parents.

When she got home, there was still nobody there, so she went straight to bed.

When she woke up she soon realised that she was not in her house or her body!

She frantically ran around the house, hoping it was all a huge, horrendous dream.

Rose Brown (11)
Kettlethorpe High School, Wakefield

THE GLITCH

Cara was in her room getting ready for bed when all of a sudden she heard something in the garden. She went to go see what it was. Cara saw a movement in the garden. Cara went down into the garden to see what the movement was. Cara screamed in terror. She couldn't believe her eyes. She hesitated and stood in fear. There was a spooky zombie in her garden. Cara screamed in fear as the zombie pulled her by the neck and pulled her into the bushes. Hundreds of people she thought she knew were trapped in small cages.

Mia Navin (14)
Kettlethorpe High School, Wakefield

THE GLITCH

Flight 2907 took off. It soared into the sky as normal. It was too normal. Then, as if in a video game, the plane started to glitch. Bright colours flashed. Eerie noises beeped. Then, some people just started fading away. I was paralysed with disbelief. Gradually, as time passed, more things were fading through walls into a white pit of absolute nothingness.

A bright beam is approaching us now. Are we in a simulation? This is not normal. Normal is not this. The beam is quickly approaching. Help. Please.

Thomas Gill (11)
Kettlethorpe High School, Wakefield

THE GLITCH

I woke up and got changed for school. I walked over to my mirror. I didn't move but my reflection did. I reached out my arm and touched the mirror. Suddenly, the mirror started sucking me in and I found myself on another planet. It was a jungle-like place with creatures of all different shapes and sizes. I started to panic. I explored the place trying to figure out how to get back home. Luckily, I found a friendly alien who made a potion for me. I drank the potion and found that I was back in my bedroom.

Anabel Gerrard (12)
Kettlethorpe High School, Wakefield

THE MAZE

Hello, my name is Kelly Wilson, and this is my story of how I got kidnapped. It was around 9.30am. I was getting ready to go out and was doing make-up. When I was at town, I felt like I was being watched. I was feeling light-headed so I went home. Then I came down this dark alleyway and then I couldn't see what was going to happen to me.

A man whispered to me and said, "You will be stuck here forever if you don't complete the maze! Level one, two, three, four!"

What was I to do?

Bryony-Jade Donnelly (11)
Kettlethorpe High School, Wakefield

THE DEVIL

George Brown was sitting on the sofa watching Rugby at his home in Jamaica when he received a phone call. An unknown voice said, "If you don't come to me today at eleven o'clock I will get four big strong people to kill you. I will message you with a location." George was scared of the four big strong men. He received a message to go to the school, collected the gun, returned home and put in a safe. He received ten thousand pounds for burying the weapon, which he used for a robbery.

Johnathon Wade-lavell (13)
Kettlethorpe High School, Wakefield

THE OTHER UNIVERSE

One sunny morning, I was just drawing: aliens, cyborgs and futuristic things. I don't know why, I was just bored. Suddenly, out of nowhere, I felt the ground shake and the walls collapse. *What's going on?* I thought. It was just me in the house at that time so I was petrified, not knowing what to do. A portal was coming from the ground like it was trying to swallow everything. It got me. All the images I drew were starting to come to life. Where was I? *This is all strange.*

Daisy Nother (12)
Kettlethorpe High School, Wakefield

THE ATTACK OF ADOLF HITLER

It was a sunny day and a boy called Daniel Done was at the beach with his friend Jeff. As they were at the beach a jet plane zoomed to England to attack us. Everyone was scared but Daniel and Jeff weren't. They ran to their house. When they got there, they geared up and readied for battle. When they got back to the beach, everything was damaged and a man stepped out of the jet. It was Adolf Hitler. Daniel and Jeff ran at him with their swords. They were too good for Hitler. Then he died.

Harry Tolson (11)
Kettlethorpe High School, Wakefield

UNTITLED

The homesickness began to kick in. I had been on a plane for twenty-two hours to Australia when suddenly there was a massive burst of darkness. The plane went pitch black. Water started to flood into the plane. We hurried out and ended up on a deserted island. The rest of the passengers were worried and restless.

After two hours a woman in a green coat suggested getting the metal from the plane and making boats to escape.

After a day the boats were ready.

We got home and then...

Annie Gittins (13)
Kettlethorpe High School, Wakefield

UNTITLED

A robot called Terry woke up in the morning and, to his surprise, there was a time machine. Not knowing what it was, he stepped into it. He landed in a different country and he was shocked because there was an active warzone. He had to fight in the war. He was stuck. He could not escape this war; he had to fight. The robot was frightened. He got his gun and started to fight the enemies. Later on, he got shot and died. Lying down on the sandy-yellow grass, he closed his eyes and said goodbye...

Ehsan Nadim (11)
Kettlethorpe High School, Wakefield

TIME IS RUNNING OUT

It was one cold, misty night in New York and there was a young woman named Lucy. She was a scientist. She finally got home and turned the TV on. She kept switching channels but there was only one thing on the news and it wasn't good! There was a terrible unknown disease and people were dropping by the minute. There was only one option and time was running out. She had to bomb New York. Two days later, she finally got her hands on a bomb. She dropped it on the city. Everything went silent.

Beth Telford (11)
Kettlethorpe High School, Wakefield

RESURRECTION OF REFLECTION

I didn't move, but my reflection did. I rushed out of the door because I was late for work, but as I left, I saw a foot and finger crawl around my mirror frame. Startled, I hurried out of my village hut to get to work.

It was when I was walking down the rocky road that someone whispered to me, I spun around to observe what appeared to be a clone of myself. I ran to find my friends to tell them that there was a psycho on the loose. But, they said that I was the dictating psychopath.

Lily Dixon (12)
Kettlethorpe High School, Wakefield

THE GLITCH

I was walking my dog through a field of daisies. Ahead of me, I saw a necklace glistening in the distance. Slowly I crept up to it wondering why it was there and if it was a sign. Months earlier, my mum had died. I lost a part of me. I grabbed the necklace and put it on. Suddenly I got transported to a place I'd never seen before. Hours later, I discovered I was 5 months in the past. I saw my mum and quickly hid. It was the 23rd of August 2024. The day before she died at 9:30 at night.

Annabel Senior (13)
Kettlethorpe High School, Wakefield

UNTITLED

I had just about had enough of trying to fix the time machine. I was beginning to think there was no hope after two years of trying, when suddenly I saw the flicker of lights and heard the roar of the engine. In the blink of an eye, I was transported to a destination I never wanted to be in, the caveman years. My hands were shaking as I tried to start the machine again but nothing was happening, no signs of life at all, not even a flicker! Was I stuck here forever with no way out at all?

Macy Grayson (13)
Kettlethorpe High School, Wakefield

THE POSSESSION

Libby and I stared at my journal. We were messing about in the forest we were documenting. Except the drawing predicted the future. Animals around us stood on their back legs, eyes like holes in their skulls. Were they possessed? They seemed it. Me and Libby shoved our things away, getting up from our knees. We didn't know what to do. Where would we go? Who would we go to? We ran as fast as our legs could take us. We were lost. Thankfully, Libby found a thorny exit. We ran and ran.

Charlotte Hardiman (12)
Kettlethorpe High School, Wakefield

THE END!

Ignoring the warnings I downloaded the app. Suddenly Kabab fell asleep, she woke up in a dark empty spot. She found her way out of one room, just to find herself in another. She was terrified. She started seeing black figures, but she learned to live with the changes until she got too stressed. Finding herself continually escaping from things following her and trying to kill her, she saw one of the figures and didn't try to escape. She died screaming in pain.

Reis Barnsley (11)
Kettlethorpe High School, Wakefield

THE GLITCH

Suddenly, I woke up and I found myself in a cartoon. There were all sorts of characters, like Scooby-Doo and the Simpsons. I thought I was in a dream, but I could feel pain and confusion about how this was happening to me. Everything was a cartoon. It looked like I was in a video game and I was in the future. Everything was different. There were flying cars. I was confused and I thought it was cool at the same time.

William Tebbutt (11)
Kettlethorpe High School, Wakefield

HALO

Everywhere is abandoned and nearly everyone is dead. This is because of an alien invasion and they are trying to attack a man-made planet (giant weapon) so they can destroy Earth. UNSC defended Earth as best they could but the aliens still got on and destroyed most of humanity. Masterchief, Spartans and Marines keep destroying them, but they keep coming. It seems like that until...

Mason Padgett (11)
Kettlethorpe High School, Wakefield

THE WAY BOB DESTROYED THE OMNIVERSE

One day a normal boy called Bob was playing in the garden with a ball. The ball popped because they thought that stabbing it with a knife was a good idea. They asked a random guy if they could have a ball so he gave them one. When Bob took the ball he became the ball. They were all shaken by what happened except the man...

Hayden Bushby (11)
Kettlethorpe High School, Wakefield

GLITCHY PIXELS

In a flash of pixels, Sam found himself within the game, his room transformed into a surreal battleground. The final level lay before him, ominous and foreboding. A towering boss loomed, its edges flashing with coded malice. Determination fuelled Sam's every move as he evaded attacks, discovering glitchy weaknesses in the boss's patterns. Adrenaline surged as the victory seemed within reach. With a final burst of courage, he unleashed an unexpected combo, exploiting the glitch. The boss shattered into digital shards, the room flickered, and Sam emerged, panting but triumphant, back in his room. The glitch had become his victorious path.

Evie Ralph (14)
Ormiston Forge Academy, Cradley Heath

DEATH HOUSE

Tick! Tock!
The clock ticked on until *ding-dong!*
A shiver of fear went down her spine. The door slowly opened as she edged nearer. "Ahhh!" the girl screamed at what she saw.
The girl circled the room facing a man.
"You're early," said Jeffy. Blood splattered on the floor from the knife he was holding. He stood still then and charged at the girl. A scream echoed in the room as Jeffy pulled the knife out of her. She dropped to the floor, tears pouring out of her eyes. She now knows not to trespass on private property again.
She died slowly and painfully.

Scarlett Reece (12)
Ormiston Forge Academy, Cradley Heath

THE GLITCH

First, their world went black. No one knew what happened. As the sound of a car crash startled him awake, the commotion got his mind thinking. *There was never any commotion in Electromedia.* One of the heroes of the interwebs would had stopped the crash. Electromedia, the home of the hero of this tale, Antivirus, was a utopia across the internet. The Electromedians were oblivious to the fact that there was some otherworldly being among them. The Glitch devoured everyone and everything in its path, vanquishing their world's best warriors. However, our hero, Antivirus, was Electromedia's only hope.

Yusuf Tekdal (12)
Ormiston Forge Academy, Cradley Heath

THE GIRL FROM THE MIRROR

I didn't move but my reflection did, staring back at me through my little bathroom mirror... A few moments after her mum had left, a little girl named Lucie found herself gazing at the reflection of her in the bathroom mirror. Creeping closer in, the girl realised that her reflection had moved but she had stopped. Confused, Lucie went to take a closer look... The girl in the mirror began crawling out and to Lucie's surprise, the girl exclaimed, "I'm your twin!"
"No, you can't be," said Lucie. But after this strange encounter, Lucie was never to be seen again...

Clarissa Ward (11)
Ormiston Forge Academy, Cradley Heath

ONE

Every clock had stopped, and every person was dead apart from me, Ava, and my two friends, Adam and May.
We were living the life at first: driving cars, raiding shops. But all good things must come to an end as we started to have the symptoms: depression, crying and many more.
Adam almost committed suicide just like the others, but we found the cure: this plant not far from London. The 'Stopper' was its name.
We found the plant, ate some straight away and collected the rest.
We decided to save the other survivors. Well, that's if there were any left.
One found.

Poppy Rydes (11)
Ormiston Forge Academy, Cradley Heath

THE ENCHANTED FOREST

Lindsay, a brave girl, was searching around an enchanted forest when something unexpected happened...
The sun hadn't risen in five years and she couldn't fix it. What could she do? Could this be solved? She looked around for any evidence of how to fix it.
Suddenly, she found a letter under a rock saying she had to do many quests to sort out what was happening to the sun. Lindsay found another girl called Courtney stranded in the forest. They began to help each other to get past the quests.
When they had finished the quests, they realised it was a big trap...

Kyrah-Louise Leighton (12)
Ormiston Forge Academy, Cradley Heath

BITTERSWEET REVENGE

Rain hammered relentlessly beneath me as I hurriedly buried the corpse. No one would ever know. It was the best plan. "Quick! Let's go before someone ventures here," whispered one of my commanders. I nodded in response. Who buries their brother you may ask? A person who wants wealth, power and strength.

A week later, we buried it but it was back... Its body stood right in front of me, blood scattered everywhere and oozing out of his limbs, fully staining his clothes, bloody red. It was as horrifying as banshees haunting a graveyard. How was it back? Why was it back?

Syeda Fatima (12)
Ormiston Forge Academy, Cradley Heath

MY MENTAL LIFE

The sun hasn't risen for five years. I have lived in this eternal darkness. It is dangerous outside, full of zombies. You'll get used to the noise soon. Day and night, though I don't even know what it looks like anymore. Mum and Dad are gone, never to return. The sun shone, then disappeared. It's said that it was toxic, and then that day, many grieved. I hope and pray that this torment ends soon, but it has never been answered. I've always felt alone, even when people were alive. Just me, the zombies and the darkness, taking over my mental health.

Sidrah Marwa (11)
Ormiston Forge Academy, Cradley Heath

UNTITLED

Once upon a time, there was a boy called Jamie. He was into computing and making games. One day at school, Jamie was walking around the school hallway and saw a poster which said, "Win £10,000 from making the best video game." So Jamie had an idea.

When the school day finished, he rushed home, opened up his laptop and started making the game. He called it, 'The Glitch'. It was meant to solve the error in the game. Once the day came, he presented the game at school. The teachers were surprised, but when the teachers tried it, it glitched.

Jasmeet Singh (11)
Ormiston Forge Academy, Cradley Heath

THE MISTAKE

Another Thursday. Lola had science first period. Poppy (her friend) noticed that Mr Jaar kept on checking the room next door. Poppy was speaking to Lola about Mr Jarr and decided to investigate at lunch but Poppy realised that she had to go for an appointment. Period three. Lola was on her own. At lunch, Lola went to the staffroom in the science block. She found a cloth with something under it. She was tempted. Lola found a mirror. She stopped. Frozen. Lola stopped but her reflection didn't. Her reflection jumped out. What will happen next? Nobody knows what.

Fatima Ateeq (12)
Ormiston Forge Academy, Cradley Heath

THE GLITCHED ROOMMATE

The sun hadn't risen for five years and mutants ruled.
April, 2211 - I met my roommate. His face was charming
and his smile shined like a thousand suns.
"Hey." The voice he spoke in was the prettiest thing I've
heard.
After that, everything sped past us like cars on a motorway.
Our first kiss was a month after we met.
Five months ago, I found out that I'm pregnant. I ran to his
room to find that he wasn't wearing any trousers and I saw
it. He had a cat tail!
We're past the challenges, even expecting a baby boy.

Harriet Brazier-Adams (11)
Ormiston Forge Academy, Cradley Heath

THE GLITCHED

Suddenly I was travelling through time. A portal whirring behind me. The sounds... Someone says my name. My breathing slows down and my eyes faint as I start to move, not keeping up with my feet. I run... I fall. Then I'm caught. A glitched robotic voice speaks to me. I'm not able to understand it, but I know it is distressed. It speaks again, begging for me to understand when I can. Its voice and what it said, I don't remember.

It took me to a place, a glitched area. The sky was black and full of green and red. I'm awoken.

Amelie Starns (11)
Ormiston Forge Academy, Cradley Heath

CHAPTER ONE: I TURNED INTO AN ANGEL

The tick and tock of the clock ticked. I was dodging and dribbling past the opposite team. A million thoughts orbited in my head. The spinning and churning of it made me feel under pressure. Strange voices told me to stop. No, give up. It's not worth it. You're not good enough. But I fought back. I told the voices, "No, I won't give up. You're not going to stop me. This is who I am and this is what I'll be."
Then I felt a gush of wind circle me up weightlessly into the air. I told myself, "Was I dreaming?"

Lara Bowater-Jones (12)
Ormiston Forge Academy, Cradley Heath

THE FIRST DEAD

I didn't move, but my reflection did. I didn't blink, but it did. Arose, I wanted it gone. That mirror, the same mirror that nearly put me through a near-death experience. My hatred for it grew stronger and stronger by the minute. I had no trance in me, I was practically worthless, nothing to live for. Why did you ruin my life? I fell to the floor, draining my eyes out. I made my decision. I was going to shatter that mirror before it killed me. Immediately, I launched the mirror out of the window. Suddenly, someone came across it.

Aleena Zeeshan (12)
Ormiston Forge Academy, Cradley Heath

POWER GENERATOR

Every clock had stopped...
I saw my life flash before my eyes. My body went cold. I'm awake again. Is this a loop?
Here I am walking down the road to my school, again. Today I'm going to try and escape this hell. But how?
Here I am at these decrepit and rusty gates at this barren wasteland, known as a school. Schools are supposed to be educational. But this one seems to be some sort of power generator, which may be why I am so drawn to it!
Every time I die, I become reincarnated. I need to escape this hell!

Oliver Earp (12)
Ormiston Forge Academy, Cradley Heath

THE DRAWING...

The drawing predicted the future. Hazel gets out of her seat, asking to switch with the girl in front of her. While sitting down, she opens the window noticing a piece of paper beside her. A picture of a plane crash... Startled, she shakes it off relaxing in her seat. Thirty minutes in, her eyes capture another drawing. A pilot asleep... What could this mean? An eerie silence went on for an hour. Goosebumps rose from her arms as a tingle of fear raced upon her neck like a car on the motorway. That's when it finally hit her.

Lilly Priest (12)
Ormiston Forge Academy, Cradley Heath

WWIII: THE SOLDIER WHO NEVER CAME HOME

Every clock had stopped. I was on a plane to France as Adolf Hitler was alive again and was invading France. On the way there, the man next to me was looking sad, so I started chatting with him, exchanging names and interests. The plane had just landed in Paris. Immediately, guns fired. We all sprinted off the plane to reach the trench. Many days went by with friends but mainly comrades. The chap who was next to me was called Johnny. We got out to raid a German base. There were guns and bombs were everywhere when *bang!*

Mac Sefton (11)
Ormiston Forge Academy, Cradley Heath

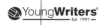

THE DAY I GOT STUCK IN A DOLL

Suddenly, I was travelling through time... Before I knew it, I was standing helplessly in the doll that looked like me. How had this happened? Am I ever going to get out? Only one hour ago, I was skipping happily through the snowy streets of Cradley Heath. The steam on the googly eyes affected my sight, all I could make out were hundreds of dolls that might be normal children whose lives were now over. I couldn't move and I couldn't scream for help. All of a sudden, the oak door opened. A girl. Will she end up like me?

Summer Woods (12)
Ormiston Forge Academy, Cradley Heath

TIME AUTOMATICALLY STOPPED

Charlie downloaded an app to win a prize but he had to go on an island with a mysterious creature. He went on the island but didn't know the powers invested on the island. When you stepped on the island, time stopped. He wandered the island. The creature never noticed him until he tried to escape. Then the creature summoned a force field. Charlie is now stuck and isn't going anywhere. He is stuck so he now stays on this island forever. He goes in the house on top of the hill. Who knows what will happen next to Charlie?

Archie Bosworth (11)
Ormiston Forge Academy, Cradley Heath

BEYOND THE GLITCH

If I had one penny for every time a strange portal popped into existence in my room, I would have two. Strange, isn't it? Certainly isn't a normal Monday morning for me! The rain was unforgiving and violently beating against my window, like a raging herd of bulls rampaging. Though I shifted my glare away from the rain and back to my phone, something caught my interest. A flicker of light approaching from above, I looked up and saw a young girl fall through the portal and hit my bed with a thud. Not what I expected.

Summer Vanes (15)
Ormiston Forge Academy, Cradley Heath

THE GLITCH

Ignoring the warnings, I downloaded the app. I am Antonio.
My two friends, Harvey and William, and I loved coding. I
found an app on the dark web. I made a game on the app.
We locked villains of the game, cartoxes, in an indestructible
crate. There was a crack in my walls.
One day, the cartoxes emerged out of my bedroom walls
and they turned Harvey into a statue. I remembered I had
created an anti-cartox machine and I turned it on. Dead
carcasses of cartoxes, but we lost our beloved friend,
Harvey. Never forgotten.

Dawood Younis
Ormiston Forge Academy, Cradley Heath

UNTITLED

It was as Monday. The clocks in our school kept us in the future. The teachers kept an eye on them after a past bombing happened. I was in maths and then heard a scream. The school got put on lockdown. The clocks stopped and everyone panicked. I then realised a student was the influenced bomber. With only a few hours left, I asked everyone but only one person caught my eye. My best friend, because earlier, she tackled me harshly so I pushed her off. I ran to the evacuated school to reset the clocks but she was there.

Keeley Jade Drake (12)
Ormiston Forge Academy, Cradley Heath

LOCKED UP IN SCHOOL

"No, please don't," I cried. "I need to go home. No!"
I felt devastated. Did I do something to deserve this?
Light flickered from a mile away. I panicked as I grabbed my phone out of my front pocket. Why won't it work?
I soon realised I had to use it in geography, then it turned off soon after.
Through my directions, light peered out of a window. I hesitated. Should I do something risky?
It was a struggle to get out, but soon I ran through a deep, dark alleyway.

Amal Ghaleb (11)
Ormiston Forge Academy, Cradley Heath

THE GAMER'S WORLD

Ignoring the warnings, I downloaded the app. All the adverts, all the pop-ups, they were all about this one game. Phone in hand, I raised my finger and placed it down on the delicate screen. I felt a tingle run through my hand, my arm, my veins. Through every part of my body. My limbs became lighter as I felt my eyes close. I tried to resist it, but I knew I was long, long, gone. I couldn't feel anything in my body. Everything had stopped. I was mindless and should have been dead. I was lost, far away.

Perry Sheldon (11)
Ormiston Forge Academy, Cradley Heath

EVERY CLOCK HAD STOPPED

Every clock had stopped... I had woken up in the morning, eating breakfast at the table on my phone making YouTube videos. Then suddenly, I looked at the time because I was going out with friends at 11 o'clock. but it was still 7am. I was shocked so I went back to bed for three hours. I woke up and it looked really dark so I checked the time and it was still 7am. I called my friends and they said the same thing. How is it still 7am? Then... suddenly, everything had stopped in existence before my eyes.

Jayden Such (12)
Ormiston Forge Academy, Cradley Heath

THE SECRETS WITHIN THE GLOOMY TOWN

Five years and still no sun to be seen. June 19th, a figure suddenly appeared in our town with his hood up, so you couldn't see his face. I was thirteen at the time and was walking past the house that he had rented me. Being my nosy self, I walked up to his slightly cracked window. His face was covered in scars. He looked pale and had grey eyes. I jumped. He saw me. I quickly sprinted back home and the next day, he was nowhere to be seen and the sun was gone. It had disappeared forever.

Alexa Marshall (11)
Ormiston Forge Academy, Cradley Heath

THE BLOOD-CURDLING SCREAM!

One day, a young boy called Charlie set off to do his normal trip to school. But that's when he went a different way and was teleported to an abandoned train. He woke up feeling dizzy, but he ignored that and carried on exploring. That's when he heard a blood-curdling scream from the back of the train. He got a huge fright when he saw the black figure gallop away. After that, he went and tried to get through the door, but he couldn't. He had to complete a quiz. He escaped.

Liam Darby (13)
Ormiston Forge Academy, Cradley Heath

THE MYSTERY OF 2000

I woke up at 5am and decided to explore a forest close to
my house. I got out my clothes and I slowly put on my boots.
I picked up a torch as it was still dark. The year is 2000.
I got into the forest when something startled me. I ran but
then quickly tripped over a rock. I found an abandoned shed
that I just had to explore!
When I checked it out, it was daylight. But when I left, it was
midnight. I had only been inside for five minutes. No one
knows what happened...

Ruby Kite (11)
Ormiston Forge Academy, Cradley Heath

THE YEAR...

"You're early," said Death. "What happened?"
Wait, I'm back. But I died. Oh, I remember, I was floating up in the clouds. Death said he was washing everyone's brains, and we would now be a random person on Earth. But he forgot to wash mine. I took a breath in. Mmm... vanilla.
"Enjoying our new flavoured air, sweetie?"
Flavoured air? Wait a minute!
"What year is it?"
"2097 honey, you must have forgotten, ha-ha!"
All of a sudden, I started floating.
"Welcome back," said Death.
"Wait, I'm back?" Confusion struck all over my body. What happened?
"Did I die again?"

Kate O'Mahony (11)
Sacred Heart Grammar School, Newry

MY BEST FRIEND...

My mirror was showing me something! My brother Jude and my best friend Elijah... I thought nothing of it, yet...
"I'm going to go and see Elijah!" I managed.
Elijah was waiting patiently at our spot. He grinned. "Nice to see you too!"
I ignored him. We wandered off somewhere... wasn't really paying attention.
"Here's a tip, friend," he stammered. "Never follow strangers down dark alleys alone..." He smirked. I was petrified! I turned my head to see Jude... He was tied up, bleeding, gone.
"Jude! Jude!" I shrieked hysterically, when blood came pouring down my forehead! It was my blood...

Kate Toner (11)
Sacred Heart Grammar School, Newry

GLITCH PRONE

'Do you wish to download the app?'

Curiously, Arwin clicked 'okay'. His phone levitated. Bewildered, he grasped it. Suddenly, he felt a plummeting sensation.

Bang! The impact rattled his lean frame. *Oh no, another glitch!* He processed his surroundings. Robots roamed the streets, and UFOs drifted over futuristic buildings. Petrified, Arwin backed into the shadows. A beep pierced his ears. He was encircled by a swarm of robots. A laser beam burned his chest, and everything went black...

He woke in a pool of sweat. It was only a nightmare. His phone pinged: 'Do you wish to download the app?'

Isabella Healy (12)
Sacred Heart Grammar School, Newry

PIRATE ASSASSIN

"You're early," said Death. "What happened?"
One day earlier... I reached the porthole and slipped my
dagger into the catch. I climbed into the cell. It stank of
blood.
"Chloe," I whispered. "We have to go now."
"Yes, but why did you do it?"
"I'll explain later," I replied. Chloe climbed out and sat on my
raft. I was about to climb out when there was an explosion.
No! I thought. *She's found me!* I grasped for my cutlass.
Suddenly, she appeared. The princess' ghost. The princess I
had killed. And that is how I am here now... in Hell.

Megan Bottell (11)
Sacred Heart Grammar School, Newry

ROVER AND THE WITCH

Every clock had stopped. My baby brother stopped crying, his sad, tear-stained face frozen. My mum's stressed face was frozen. The rain had stopped. I felt a shiver behind me, almost like a ghost had touched me. It's back; he was back. I can't stand him.

"Did you miss me?" he said, a wide grin spreading across his face.

"Before you ask, no, I'm not doing it. Why do you still bother asking?"

His grin had vanished, and he answered, "Sarah, you're a witch, and you can't deny it, but that's not why I'm here."

Rover answered, "Tiarnan, he's alive!"

Lauren Cumiskey (12)
Sacred Heart Grammar School, Newry

THE MYSTERIOUS BOX

Every clock had stopped. Mum and Nan had stopped, everything and everyone had frozen and were blurring away.
Earlier today: "Rachel!" shouted Mum. "Your nan's here!"
I was slightly shocked. We never saw Nan much now that Dad was working in Australia.
"Here," said Nan, handing me a box. Mum nudged me.
"Thank you," I muttered, taking the mysterious box. I took it up to my room and set it beside my cards. It was my birthday and I had turned twelve. Suddenly, it glowed and shook violently. I ran over to it and opened it. Then everything went black.

Cara Cunningham (12)
Sacred Heart Grammar School, Newry

THE REFLECTION

I awoke again due to another horrendous nightmare, except this one was different; really different. I woke, panting, quaking and sweating. Dreaming of my own reflection calling out to me wasn't the twisted part, 'twas my distorted and drooping face. All I could remember after was being sucked into the mirror by grappling, elongated claws. Thinking of it upsets my thought processing over everything. I climbed out of the bed keeping me hostage to these dreams. I debated looking at my mirroring self. I was taken aback at the black holes gazing. "Did you enjoy your performance?" Suddenly, I couldn't breathe.

Liadán Farrell (13)
Sacred Heart Grammar School, Newry

THE ROGUE REFLECTION

"What!" I exclaimed. "How is this possible?"
I was completely still, not moving at all, but my reflection was. It was dancing and skipping around, but the entire time, it kept its eyes on me.
"This must be a dream! This has to be a dream! Reflections don't move by themselves!"
I pinched myself, silently praying that I would wake up in my warm, safe bed, and laugh it off. I didn't.
"No," I whispered, trembling, desperately reaching out to try and grasp something to steady me.
My reflection laughed, "How silly. I've always been moving. You just never noticed."

Ellen McGivern (12)
Sacred Heart Grammar School, Newry

KING COBRA

It is as normal a day as any I'm on the sofa with my sister looking for something on TV. Out of curiosity, I switch on the news. "Warning! Serious apocalypse called King Cobra has started. Stay at home!" the reporter announces. Extremely shocked, we run to the window to look outside; snakes everywhere. They just keep coming! "We need to call Mum, she could be in serious danger!" Stella calls out.
I take the phone. "It's dead..." I say, panicking. We flee to lock all the doors, not forgetting about the windows.
We reassure each other, "It'll be okay..."

Laura Syrokosz (12)
Sacred Heart Grammar School, Newry

THE POKELINGO OF DEATH

I was terrible at my languages so I downloaded Pokelingo, a language app. Worst mistake ever. *Beep!* "Come on, it's 3am!" I spoke. I read it and I was shocked. 'Learn French... or else?' I read. Suddenly, all my apps turned into Pokelingo! I quickly tried to delete it. It worked! At least, I thought it did until... *Beep!* "Nooo!" I screamed as I read the notification. It said, 'Let's see what happens when you try to delete me.' Next thing I know, all I see is Pokelingo's white eyes. That's when I realised I was done. Pokelingo killed me.

Sinead McAllister (11)
Sacred Heart Grammar School, Newry

POISONOUS PEN

9C had science as their first class yesterday. Tiana went to the first class and clumsily lost her pen. She found a mysterious pen on the floor and began using it. The class became very boring and frustrating as their teacher was very agitating, so she drew pictures of her teacher with a zip on their mouth. Then, *bam!* The teacher's mouth was glued! She muffled but nothing came out. Her teacher fell and fainted. Then the pen levitated and started drawing Tiana with a hair removal potion. Tiana uncontrollably picked up the potion and, *boom!* She was bald. She was utterly bewildered.

Carragh McShane (12)
Sacred Heart Grammar School, Newry

OÁVATOS

I heard of this app called Oávatos that tells you the date you will die. I thought it was just to scare kids, so I downloaded it as a joke. But when I opened it, I started worrying but I did it anyway because I thought I was just being a baby.
'What's your name?' a box on the screen appeared.
I typed 'Kat'.
'No, it's not' was written on the screen and another appeared, 'Kathy'. I typed wondering how it knew my name. A lone hourglass appeared and after a few seconds the screen said, '23/2/12'. "That's tomorrow!"

Lucy Doran (11)
Sacred Heart Grammar School, Newry

RUNAWAY

I felt my fingers slide against the latch; my feet stepped forward. I was out. I started walking hesitantly. As I approached the end of the street, I heard a familiar voice calling my name. "Ella! Get back here this instant!" It was Mother. I didn't listen. I kept walking briskly. Pretending I couldn't hear. The shouts got louder. Father was shouting too. I hitched my skirt and began to run. I heard Mother calling me louder. Father ran to me faster.

Father caught up, holding my shoulder. "Ella! What is the meaning of this?" he cried.

I gulped, fidgeting...

Aoife Hayes (11)
Sacred Heart Grammar School, Newry

THE BURDEN OF TIME

Ignoring the warnings, I downloaded the app. It said *'Click here'*. I clicked *'1912'* as a joke. I closed my eyes. I was in Cork suddenly. I saw the Titanic. I grabbed my phone and clicked out of the app and shut my eyes. I was back in my room. Me being there did something though. I blocked Harold Lowe from boarding. He saved four people, so some people didn't exist. I opened the app and clicked *'2016'* (the current year). I saw myself downloading the app. My past self looked at me, screamed, then disappeared. Then I slowly vanished...

Molly Keenan (11)
Sacred Heart Grammar School, Newry

THE BEACH

I was at the beach with my friends. They suggested we all go into the water. We all went in.

"Help!" I screamed. But my voice was muffled by the water. Something pulled my ankle. Its claws were digging into me. When I got near the surface, it dragged me down again. I was drowning!

Everything went black. Suddenly, I woke up to my friends saying, "Let's go into the water!"

I must be dreaming, I thought. But I wasn't! No matter what I did, I couldn't escape. The same moment kept repeating itself over and over again. I was trapped.

Aine McQuaid (12)
Sacred Heart Grammar School, Newry

FREEZE!

I woke up to find the paperboy frozen outside my house. I rushed out of bed to realise time had *frozen!* I snapped my fingers. *Boom!*

Time unfroze, then I snapped them again and - *silence!* Time had frozen. I ran outside across the road and then swapped the paperboy's newspaper for an egg, then snapped my fingers. *Whoosh!* The paperboy threw an egg at my neighbour instead of the paper. I snapped my fingers, then I laughed as I realised how much fun this could be. I snapped my fingers once again but...

Uh-oh. Time was *frozen!*

Orlaith McCoy (12)

Sacred Heart Grammar School, Newry

THE ALGAE MAN

Reports of the algae are on every channel. We're expecting it. Dad's packing our bags and loading them into our van. We don't know where to go. Boats have stopped docking, planes have stopped flying and hotels have shut down. Our phones keep ringing from anonymous callers and it feels like there's a chill in the air. Suddenly, the powerlines spark and out electric goes out. It's pitch black. Then, just like they had sparked before, our powerlines spark and our electic comes on. Standing across from our house is a figure, which seems to be made of gloopy algae.

Nora McCusker (12)
Sacred Heart Grammar School, Newry

THE SHADOW SWITCH

Beth got bullied and her only friend was her reflection. Walking to school one day, Beth noticed that her reflection wasn't there. She thought nothing of it. But the next day, her reflection was holding a doll (which wasn't in her hand). All the other shadows were holding dolls as well. People were going missing! It didn't take her long to realise the dolls were voodoo dolls! The shadows were getting revenge after humans made them follow them around and do all the things we do. Those people did bully Beth, her reflection was her best friend. So she let them disappear.

Genevieve Lennon (11)
Sacred Heart Grammar School, Newry

THE ARTIST WHOSE WILDEST DREAMS CAME TRUE!

Hello, my name is Anna. I am twelve years old. I had a dream to become an artist. I was thinking of what drawing to do next. *How about the Earth, but in a different version*, I thought to myself... I drew crisp, burnt grass lying along the outer shell of the Earth. The news read: 'Something terrible has happened to our beautiful Earth. We have astronauts on their way to find out what's happening.' I furiously scribbled on my page. The crusty grass, loads of water overflowing over the river.
"Hmmm, it wouldn't be my drawing. Would it be..."

Amy Harper (11)
Sacred Heart Grammar School, Newry

APP DRAGON

Dismissing the warnings, I installed the app. Sighing, I decided to walk instead of aimlessly waiting. Halfway through, I heard a crackle and felt an urge to go back. I rushed home worrying. There was nothing new except for the icon on my screen. I clicked on the app and searched up 'dragon'. Immediately, a reel of realistic pictures appeared. I smiled, satisfied. This app really does generate phenomenal photos! I chose the one of the dragon with flowers. I clicked and there was a crackle! I looked around, startled, and there was the tiny dragon, tumbling over a flower.

Evelyn Joan Kennedy (11)
Sacred Heart Grammar School, Newry

LEAVE HER ALONE

Gretta was a normal girl. Well, that's what it seemed like. She was very self-obsessed and wasn't very popular. She was popular with someone though, her reflection. Everything she did, her reflection copied, as it should, until something strange happened. Every mirror she looked at shattered. She tried to leave all this chaos, but the mirrors followed her. All of her reflections were after her, like an army. She decided just to suck it up and look at them. She turned around, the lights shut off, and the mirrors grabbed her into them. She was trapped forever and ever...

Hannah Begley (12)
Sacred Heart Grammar School, Newry

THE LAST TRUTH

A man lay on the ground, unmoving but conscious, as a chill ran through the air. Not even taking a glance at where it had come from, he called out to the wind, "Hello... old friend."
A figure shrouded in darkness appeared above the man. "Sorry, but we have never met," it said in hushed whispers. "Not in this time, but I assure you we have before." The man said it with such confidence the figure had to believe him. He looked around at the wasteland that was once a thriving forest and said to Death, "It's all my fault."

Sarah McAleenan (12)
Sacred Heart Grammar School, Newry

THE HALL CHASE

I jolted out of bed. A tall, slim figure was standing over me. It was Death. I jumped out of my bed and ran to my parents' room, but the doors disappeared and turned into bricks. "Help me! Help!" I shouted, looking over my shoulder. He was still following me. I ran down the hall until my legs gave in. "Please, I'm too young to die. I have my whole life ahead of me, please!" I burst into tears. *This is it*, I thought *I'm going to die.*
Death hugged me tightly,
"Lily! Wake up!"
It was all a dream...

Niamh McShane (12)
Sacred Heart Grammar School, Newry

THE POWER OF HIDDEN TALENTS

Ellie is a 12-year-old girl who is an amazing artist. Almost everything she draws becomes reality. Everyone thought it was just a coincidence, but there were too many coincidences. Ellie drew a picture of two girls trapped in a forest. She went to meet her friend, Lily, at the forest. While there, the girls realised they were unable to find an exit. Lily lost all hope of getting out. Ellie began to draw the picture, just this time, the drawing had an exit. She quickly showed Lily.

They both looked astonished and said, "The drawings predicted the future."

Orlaith Rice (12)

Sacred Heart Grammar School, Newry

THE ENDLESS WAIT

The world is in complete darkness, or at least that's what it seems. But somewhere out there, people are dying from heat, while me and my crew of ten survivors will never see the light of day again. Nobody knows how it happened. People are going crazy; killings, cannibalism, and new religions are now the norm. We've been searching, trying to find answers that we all know will never be found. But we keep going, hanging on to the hope that tomorrow the sun will rise again. Inevitable darkness and cold freezes every part of your body; there's no escape.

Ruth-Alice McKinney (11)
Sacred Heart Grammar School, Newry

THE END OF MAYBRIDGE HIGH

"You're early," said Death. "What happened?"
My mind was still hazy, all I could remember were flashing lights, bright colours and a weird ticking noise. Then it came flooding back.
It was an ordinary Wednesday in maths when the alarm sounded. I was told to have a look outside to see if we were in danger.
Then I saw it, a big, black box with wires poking out. I immediately knew it was a bomb, and if I didn't defuse it, we would all die.
I rushed towards it and started tugging on the wires, but it was too late.

Isobel Mackin (12)
Sacred Heart Grammar School, Newry

146

MIRROR, MIRROR ON THE WALL

Jasmine was with her friends at some dinner party she had been invited to. She hated stuff like this. She would much rather be in her room, alone. They were all talking without her, so she wandered off. Her friend had a big house, then she saw it. A mirror. She stared at it, then she blinked, but her reflection's white eyes didn't. She fell back, shocked, though her reflection was still towering over her. She quickly punched the mirror, and then that thing was gone! She sighed and turned around and saw herself, with pure white eyes, smiling widely.

Ellie Mooney (11)
Sacred Heart Grammar School, Newry

147

THE SUN'S RETURN

The sun hadn't risen in five years. It was the year 2104 and a boy named Leo had a dream of saving the world. Life was different. There was no sun or school and animals were dying out. Leo woke in a dark room.

"Took you long enough," said a voice.

"How do I get home?"

"The only way out is that button, but if you do I stay here forever."

Leo thought hard and decided... "You go, I stay."

As soon as she pressed the button, Leo woke with a jolt. He looked out of his window as the sun rose...

Ava Cowan (12)
Sacred Heart Grammar School, Newry

THE DARK FOREST

One day in Trasnavalley, James went to school.
When he was coming home, he went through the forest. He always knew the forest was his happy place. James sat down but fell asleep.
When he woke up, it was pitch black. Someone was standing over him, it was a goddess.
She didn't like James being in the forest, so she got up and said, "With all the power in me, the sun won't rise, forever!"
James was shocked at what he had done. He ran home.
From that day on, the sun did not rise again. The day melted into the night.

Emma Stevenson (12)
Sacred Heart Grammar School, Newry

FIXED IN TIME

I'm Cecilia, and a year ago, something changed. I was coming home from school when the dog walkers stopped. The postman and all the cars too. Every animal froze. But not me. One minute passed and then they were moving again. I went home and asked my mum.
She said, "I haven't stopped working all day!" Odd. It happened again and again. Each time I could move, but no one else could. And each time it lasted one minute longer. A year passed and I woke up. Nothing moved. A week went by and still, nothing. Now here I am. Alone. Forever...

Eve Burke (11)
Sacred Heart Grammar School, Newry

THE UGLY TRUTH

I woke to see the same pictures I see every day. The same ugly drawings. I quickly realised that one was missing. It was the one of my neighbour being eaten by a snail-like monster! I groaned before sitting up in bed. I stood up and looked outside to see a large, thick trail of goo outside my neighbour's house. *Lizzie, what are you thinking?* I thought to myself, shaking my head, but another drawing had gone missing. This one showed a picture of the ground of my house crumbling under my feet. The ground started to crumble before collapsing...

Megan Murphy (11)
Sacred Heart Grammar School, Newry

THE APP THAT DESTROYED THE EARTH

Ignoring the warning, I downloaded the app. My name is Lilly and I've just destroyed all humankind. All I did was download an app. I didn't read the comments warning me. It was a simple app to tell me what I would look like when I was older. It also featured artificial intelligence. I woke up the next morning to find everyone looking at least seventy years older. Everyone except me. I started weeping with fear as everyone around me started to shrivel up and die right before me. It was all my fault! All humans became extinct. Everyone, except me.

Stella Padden (11)
Sacred Heart Grammar School, Newry

WHEN THE SUN STOPPED RISING

The sun hadn't risen for five years, but that was about to change. We were going to live on Mars! It would take 365 years to get there.

You may wonder, "You'd be 379! You'd die!"

They were going to give us medicine and our food would be frozen for our arrival. I was worried I wouldn't see my family again.

When we boarded the spaceship, I went into my pod and was injected with medicines. I felt myself go numb and my eyes closed.

I woke to sirens and saw a ball of fire coming towards me. I braced myself. Was this the end?

Sophie McGeeney (11)
Sacred Heart Grammar School, Newry

ALL ALONE IN THIS COLD, HARD WORLD

Ignoring the warnings, I downloaded the app...
I was suddenly transferred back into the night. I woke up feeling just like I do every morning, tired and not wanting to go to school where everyone bullied me, even my teachers because I was not one of them.
I pulled myself out of bed, got changed, and had my breakfast. It never occurred to me that my house was quiet. My family usually didn't get up until ten. I went outside and there was... nothing! No babies, no crying, no dogs barking. That was the day I found myself alone in the world.

Lucy Gribben (11)
Sacred Heart Grammar School, Newry

THE SKETCHBOOK

The drawings predicted the future. It was as if she knew it was gonna happen. Like she had already lived it before. It was scary because my little sister would always spend hours in her room drawing. We had always known that Ellie was different, Ellie predicted the future, I'm telling you! No one ever believed me when I told them, so I don't bother anymore.

It was just an ordinary day, as usual, when suddenly, my mum got the call. As we rushed out, the last thing we saw was Ellie's sketchbook. The last page had a burning school.

Aoibhin Mulligan (12)
Sacred Heart Grammar School, Newry

I NEED MORE TIME

I was five when the clocks stopped ticking. Every living thing froze, except me. At first, it was fun but all good things must come to an end. Now I'm fifteen years old and all alone. I miss my mum, friends, being comforted when I cry, having someone laugh at my jokes. Most of all, I miss my father, a respectable scientist. I remember him telling my mum he had one day left to complete his project or else his boss would fire him. *He must've been desperate,* I thought, bitterly, after seeing him putting supplies in his shopping cart...

Cara O'Hare (13)
Sacred Heart Grammar School, Newry

THE WEEK

It was just a normal day. I woke up and did my daily routine as usual, but it was the 27th of September. The next day, everything changed. When I woke up, I'd started to notice that everything was strangely familiar to yesterday, until it hit me. It was the 27th of September, the same day as yesterday.

I thought that I was hallucinating but I wasn't. School felt so weird; I knew everything!

This continued on for about a week. All I wanted was a normal day. Then it stopped. I was free! I was so happy that it was finally over!

Lena Wojciechowska (12)
Sacred Heart Grammar School, Newry

ALL THE CLOCKS STOPPED BUT SO DID EVERYONE ELSE

It happened at twelve o'clock, Mum said to go to the shop and be back by half past. So I went back and when I got there everyone had stopped. I looked at my phone, it was still twelve o'clock. I ran home, everything had stopped. But so had the clocks. Then my phone rang and I answered it. I repeat, "Hello, you have been chosen as one of the ten ten-year-olds to take part in this competition, you have twenty-four hours to save your town from execution! Because of too much population, only one person can win, good luck!"

Eve Convery (12)
Sacred Heart Grammar School, Newry

I AM NOT HER!

I didn't move but my reflection did... Getting ready in the mirror, I saw myself blink. You're not supposed to see yourself blink, right? "How did I see myself blink?" I said Then, I noticed I was smirking. No, she was smirking at me. I am not her... she is strange. Why is she staring at me? "Stop it! Stop! Stop!" I shouted. "Stop smirking at me!" I examined her closer. Her doing the same... when suddenly she grabbed me and pulled me through the mirror! I screamed but the only one that heard me was her!

Amy McLorinan (12)
Sacred Heart Grammar School, Newry

MY ROAMING REFLECTION

It was a normal day, or so I thought. In the bathroom, something unimaginable happened. I stood still, but my reflection didn't. My jaw almost hit the floor. What did this mean? Was there two of me or was I in the twilight zone? When I wanted to move, I was frozen with fear, whilst the reflection sniggered! I told my mum but for weeks, my reflection mimicked my every move. I wanted to recapture that moment but never could. Was I insane? Surely I had imagined it. Until home alone, my reflection winked when I didn't. It started again.

Chloe O'Hare (12)
Sacred Heart Grammar School, Newry

THAT'S WHEN I REALISED EVERY CLOCK STOPPED...

I awoke this morning without hearing my mother's alarm clock. As I got up and went downstairs, I had a strange feeling in my head. I walked into the kitchen and no one was moving. There was food flung in the air, but it wasn't moving. It was like it was... frozen. I went outside because I thought I could be dreaming, but then birds froze mid-flight and another and another. Then, I started thinking if everything was frozen, why wasn't I? I came inside because I was confused and that's when I realised every clock had stopped.

Fion McCrink (11)
Sacred Heart Grammar School, Newry

GOODBYE SUN

Dear Diary,
A few minutes from now, it will be five years since we started living in darkness. It started when 2023 ended and we were all partying because we were excited for the new year. When the clock struck midnight, we went to bed and woke up to complete darkness. We checked every clock in the house and they all said it was 9:30. Days went past and still no sun. All the flowers, vegetables and fruits are gone. No one knows why the sun won't rise. Another Happy New Year, so that means the sun hasn't risen in five years.

Cara Magill (11)
Sacred Heart Grammar School, Newry

THE MYSTERIOUS MIRROR

Natalie realised she needed a new mirror. She bought the mirror off a mysterious website. It came the next day but in a strange box. She was looking at it, proud of her purchase. After that, everything she was touching started to glitch. The next day her reflection started glitching. She tried to touch it but she got sucked in it. She appeared to be in a glitchy world. She saw an old staff strengthening a really glitchy tower in the world. She teleported into the tower and destroyed it. She got out of the world and destroyed the mirror.

Megan Galbraith (12)
Sacred Heart Grammar School, Newry

STRIKING TWELVE

We buried it, but it was back. I'm Danielle and this is my story. It was my 20th birthday and I got a watch. At first, it was a normal watch, but when the clock struck 12 on my birthday, I started the whole week over again. I was struck in the past.

I went to meet my friend, Izzy, but she didn't understand. She was living in the past.

I buried the watch yesterday but when I woke up this morning, it was like it was haunted.

I screamed, "It's following me!"

What will I do, I'm really scared.

Kara Leckey (12)
Sacred Heart Grammar School, Newry

TIME HAD STOPPED!

Every clock had stopped. I was waiting up in my room for dinner. I was getting hungry, so I decided to go check. My mother had her back turned so I asked, "Mum, is dinner ready yet?" She didn't answer. "Hello, Mum? Are you going to answer me?" There was a dead silence. No one was talking, not even a mouse. I went over to the TV and turned it on. My favourite show, Young Sheldon, but no one was moving. I checked the cuckoo clock. It was 10:59. I counted sixty seconds, then I suddenly realised time had stopped...

Erin McCrink (11)
Sacred Heart Grammar School, Newry

THE DARK DOWNLOAD

One dark night, I was out with some friends and told them about some app I saw. They told me that it predicts the exact time and cause of your death. "You're lying!" I said. "You're just trying to scare me." *Whatever,* I thought and went home. By the time I was home, it was 11 o'clock, and I was tired of scrolling on my phone so much, so I put on the television. As soon as I put it on, an advertisement for the app came up, so I downloaded it. I stared in horror and read '12 o'clock'!

Charlotte McGreevy (11)
Sacred Heart Grammar School, Newry

THE END... OR AT LEAST FOR HER...

"Hey, it's MJ. I got a letter from my mum saying she created an app that helps people with robots, but now they kill people. I knew it wasn't going to end well and now she's dead. I miss her, but now I have other matters to worry about, like how we're going to save everyone."
I set the recording down to go to where MJ was, the lab. Together, we went to the control room and fought against the robots. I turned off the power and deleted the app. "We finally won," I said, while holding her dead body...

Mary O'Loughlin (11)
Sacred Heart Grammar School, Newry

THE SUN IS GONE

The sun hasn't risen in five years. Hi, my name is Tracy, and I haven't been able to go outside in over five years because the stupid sun suddenly vanished one day. All humans live in glass capsules and watch the world freeze even more.

We only have a limited amount of food and water, but I heard Mum and Dad talking to each other about a shortage of food.

I asked them about it and they said people are taking other people's supplies, even killing others just to get our rations. I have no idea who I can trust now.

Ella Keenan (12)
Sacred Heart Grammar School, Newry

THE PEN AND BOOK DREW THE WORLD

One year ago a girl called Kate was born into a dark, plain world. She found a pen and book beside her campfire. Firstly, she drew a house and suddenly a house appeared. She didn't cop on that it was the one she drew. Next, she drew a dog with Buddy on his collar. Surely, a dog appeared. Then she screamed, "OMG!" and began to draw more and more stuff. She drew them smaller so she could fit more stuff onto the page. She drew trees, people, houses, light and the sky as well as oceans. Then the world was finally complete.

Melissa Moley (12)
Sacred Heart Grammar School, Newry

WHEN THE SUN CAUSED A GLOBAL FAMINE

On March 16th, we were told that the sun would rise in exactly one year. We were so relieved to hear as for the past four years, we had no sun and were going through a global famine. Our fields were flooded, and we were low on food. Our trees weren't sprouting and everything was so depressing and bleak! It didn't feel like Christmas because there was no Shloer and in my opinion, all the special drinks make Christmas!

At last, it was March 16th again! We were told it would rise at 4pm. We started counting down the seconds...

Grace Donnelly (12)
Sacred Heart Grammar School, Newry

THE PREMONITION

Although it was almost home time, I idly doodled on a paper scrap. My dark, mysterious dreams flooded the page in an array of complexion as I drew. My thoughts were foggy but the sketches were clear. Didn't think much of the crumpled page as I dragged myself home. I flopped onto my bed and threw my bag in the corner. I watched as the page tumbled out. I took one last look at it and tossed it into the spitting flames. Lights out.

I woke to the blaring noise of the fire brigade. My drawings had predicted this, the future.

Aoibheann McMahon (13)
Sacred Heart Grammar School, Newry

THE FUTURE

I got a detention today and had to clean the school library. But something strange happened. There were some drawings that told the future! But one of them seemed to have a monster, in my house! When I finished, I walked home, scared. I tried to distract myself from thinking about it, but I couldn't. I went to bed, but I couldn't sleep. I lay awake, all night, thinking about what would happen in the morning. Mum walked into my room that morning, saying she had a surprise for me. She opened the door and in ran a... dog!

Ava McIntyre (11)
Sacred Heart Grammar School, Newry

THE APP

I was just minding my own business when my phone beeped. It had a message on it, saying to download the app. So, I went into the app store but the app only had half a star and bad reviews, saying not to download it because it was dangerous.

Yet, I still got the app. When I opened the app, it was just a black screen but then a message came up. It said 'You should have listened to the reviews.'

Immediately I closed the app. Furthermore, my phone shut off. Suddenly, I realised it was all a dream. *Phew!*

Bella McCoy (12)
Sacred Heart Grammar School, Newry

THE HOUSE OF DRAWINGS

"Hi, my name's Obsidian! Want to come to my house?" I had never seen this girl before, although I didn't want to be rude, so I said yes. As we walked up to her house, I felt an odd feeling in me. Her house was dark and gloomy. Inside, there was a huge surprise. There were lots of horrifying drawings on the walls. "These are my drawings. Do you like them?" I was so confused. The scariest one was of the world, and it looked demolished and Obsidian was on top of it. Were the drawings... the future...

Sarah Main (12)
Sacred Heart Grammar School, Newry

THE WOMAN IN THE MIRROR

I stood in front of the mirror admiring myself. Today, I was getting married and it was to the most handsome man I'd ever seen. Suddenly, my reflection moved to the left and then to the right, but I didn't. Strange. Then it moved again, stared me dead in the eye and said, "I would make a much better bride than you." Before I had time to do anything, she clicked her fingers and walked away. Only after a few seconds, I realised I was no longer in the bathroom but an empty void, and my whole body was frozen.

Iga Malcher (12)
Sacred Heart Grammar School, Newry

I DIDN'T MOVE BUT MY REFLECTION DID

As my friends and I wandered down the street, we suddenly encountered an abandoned school. Hesitantly, we entered the corridor. My friends insisted that I must go into the bathrooms. I felt a surge of pressure hit me like a wave. Walking into the peculiar, gloomy bathrooms, I scanned them. A mystic mirror caught my eye. Looking into this uncanny mirror, I saw my reflection waving at me. My heart sank to my feet, my shaky hand attempted to wave back but suddenly I was grasped deep into the mirror, never to be seen again...

Elana Sheppard (12)
Sacred Heart Grammar School, Newry

THE DOWNLOADING

Ignoring the warnings, I downloaded the app. As it was loading, I was starting to rethink my decision. When I opened the app, it all seemed normal... well that's what I thought. It told me to create and print the pictures as I did them. I did my first creation. It was a monster I was wanting to create for years and when it was printed I took it out and suddenly started to move around on the paper and it popped out and grew bigger and bigger and scarier and scarier. It started breaking everything in its path, then...

Molly Coulter (12)
Sacred Heart Grammar School, Newry

JUST A GIRL AND A NOTEBOOK...

Luna sat on the ground drawing, then her bully saw her, walked up to her and tore up her notebook. Luna was devastated. The bell rang, they all went home. When Luna got home, she cried and told her mother about her bully. She felt bad, so she went to a sketchy shop and bought a notebook.

When she got back, she gave the notebook to Luna. The next day, Luna drew her bully... The bell rang, and everyone was outside, then her bully fell onto the road and got run over by a car... Just like Luna had predicted.

Cara McAteer (12)
Sacred Heart Grammar School, Newry

THE EERIE CLASSROOM

Hi, my name is Thomas and I'm about to tell you the scariest day of my life. It was once just a normal day with my mum yelling at me to get up, me stuffing toast down my mouth to get to school on time.

I got into my classroom, but nobody was there which was strange as I was usually the last one in. Just an eerie silence, then thousands of robots flew into the room shouting, "I will get you, Thomas!" I fled, hands sweating and heart pounding. I thought this was the end of my life until...

Anna McCusker (11)
Sacred Heart Grammar School, Newry

PAUSE

It started when I saw a blue remote and clicked the pause symbol. I thought it was just an old TV remote, but instead, I think it stopped the world.

I froze in fear and shock as I saw birds floating. Cars were statues, and people's hearts froze.

Then I ran into the kitchen, with my small, skinny legs and saw my dad sitting on our blue leather sofa and my mum pouring the tea for me when I came back inside. But instead of it rising in the cup, it was frozen in mid-air.

What had happened?

Sienna McAllister (12)
Sacred Heart Grammar School, Newry

UNTITLED

When I was six, I drew a picture. I don't know why. It was as if someone in my head was telling me to do it. The picture was the world in ruins. Buildings were crumbling down and there was smoke everywhere. The sky was grey and people were running away screaming. When my mum saw it, she was shocked and stood there with a horrific expression on her face. She took the picture away and I never saw it again until today. I looked out of the window. My picture had come to life. The town was in ruins.

Lucy McGrath (12)
Sacred Heart Grammar School, Newry

THE SUN MALFUNCTION

I'm Lily and I love playing on my computer. Lately, I have been using it to try to get the sun back. Today I figured it out! You wouldn't understand how I did it, so I'm not going to try explaining it. It took me a year, I'm so proud! Before I worked this out, life was dull and very dangerous. How am I going to get the project to happen though? I will have to write to NASA!

I wrote my letter and sent it. The next day, NASA phoned me and told me that the project would work!

Caitlin Morgan (11)
Sacred Heart Grammar School, Newry

THE FALLING SKY

I woke up just like any other day in this big city. I made my cup of coffee and looked out the window to find the clouds moving a lot faster than they usually do. I knew something wasn't right. Then I packed my bag and left my house. The air felt heavy. I started walking down the street and all of a sudden, the sky started falling around me. Then it went dark. Next thing, I woke up just like I usually do. It was as if nothing ever happened but it kept playing over and over in my head.

Sophie Hughes (11)
Sacred Heart Grammar School, Newry

IT CAME BACK...

We buried it but it was back. I don't know how it happened. It was my dad's one-year anniversary. I got up and put on my best clothes. It was hard not to cry but I had to get through the day.

I drove to the church and sat on the pew. The mass was sad, but I didn't cry. I came home and walked up to my room to get changed. Suddenly, I saw a familiar teddy sitting on my bed. I then realised it was the teddy that Dad had given to me when I was young. How did it get here...?

Emma Lowery (11)
Sacred Heart Grammar School, Newry

IT CAME BACK...

It was just another day in Dublin. I went to the woods with my friends. Upon arriving, I noticed an unusual doll, but I ignored it and left. When I got home, the door knocked. I opened it and saw the doll, so I decided to take it back to the woods. I thought that, if I buried it, it wouldn't come back, so that's what I did. When I got home, I went straight to bed since I was exhausted. When I woke up, the door knocked again. I opened it, but to my horror, it was back...

Yasmin Frizell (11)
Sacred Heart Grammar School, Newry

THE PE LESSON

It all started in PE. As I was running about, I took one step, and the year went back by one, then another step. I didn't notice about one hundred years had passed. All the children were well dressed in fancy dresses or suits. I continued running, hoping it was a nightmare. I ran so far that the school disappeared, buildings faded, and people too. I heard the roar of dinosaurs. I ran as far as I could bringing more animals back from the dead. I had no hope to live now.

Heidi Small (12)
Sacred Heart Grammar School, Newry

THE TIME TRAP

I was just trying to get my shopping completed so I could stay at home all week but then suddenly everything stopped. All I could see was a glitch staring back at me. It was just us. I tried to run, move away, but always got reset back to the start of my day. The more I tried, the greater it grew. I tried to lure it into my trap but it shut with a snap! Now the world is purely frozen and the glitch now rules. Nobody is safe, not even you...

Mēabh McAleavey (12)
Sacred Heart Grammar School, Newry

THE GLITCH

"You're late," said Death...
The girl stared in terror with a shiver down her spine talking to thin air.
"She's coming...!" said the innocent young girl.
"Now, she's coming now?" replied Death with an angry tone.
"Tell everyone to set off all the alarms and sirens!"
Beep. Beep. Beep. There were flashing red lights and sounds echoing, petrifying everyone there. There was a colossal amount of people trying to escape the building. Suddenly, out of nowhere, The Glitch came. "I'm looking for Katie Rose," he said with a menacing look on his face. Katie stepped forward with a lump in her throat...

Imogen Webb (11)
Tabor Academy, Braintree

REGRETTABLE MISTAKES

"You're early," said Death. "What happened?"
It was fifty years tonight since that girl disappeared. It was
the early 1970s, and Emma, Dylan, Maddie and I were
forced to go into the woods by Emma to look around. We
regrettably witnessed the town's mafia dumping a body into
the nearby lake. Someone turned their head and chased
after us. They caught Emma, handed me a gun and said,
"It's you or her." Everyone had run away, and I had to do the
unthinkable... I couldn't handle the guilt. Fifty years ago I
shot her, and now it's my turn.

Annie-Mae Dunlop (11)
Tabor Academy, Braintree

THE UPRISING

Fear rippled through my spine as a wild can of Pepsi thrust out from the bottom of the vending machine, just nanometers from crippling my face. As a crowd started to form, the vending machine glowed a shade of ominous red. Screams echoed within my pounding ears as the vending machine rattled violently and stretched its materialising metallic arms and legs. Suddenly, it shot into the sky. All I could hear now was my heart beating as colourful bottles and packets rained down. I just barely managed to dodge a storm of hailing coins before everything went black.

Tyler Webb (12)
Tabor Academy, Braintree

AGAIN?

I woke up, believing it was a normal day. I was very wrong about that. Very recently, a scientist found this... 'glitch'. It's still not clear what it does, but ever since it was discovered, I've had a feeling of deja vu every day, like every day is the exact same. Maybe the glitch had something to do with it. Regardless, I left my house and went to the forest, a magical place where I relaxed. It was all silent until I heard a crack. Looking in the direction of the sound, something odd appeared. Everything went dark, and then...

Tiegan Rudd (16)
Tabor Academy, Braintree

THE GLITCH: A DARK DEATH

The figure appeared. He was nervous but determined. He wasn't meant to be here. He was Death. The end of life personified. He drew a curved blade. It was his time. A psychotic grin grew on his face. The gods had practically enslaved him and now he would have his revenge. The glitch in nature had been his plan and as such he had little time before he's stopped. He may have begun his massacre before he would be killed. Death, beaten. But not before thousands died. He breathed in deeply before beginning to enact his violent, ruthless revenge.

Theo Warner (12)
Tabor Academy, Braintree

THE SYSTEM GLITCH

The sun hasn't risen in four years. It was 1981 when the tragedy started.

Late one night yet only but stars that showed any light and the moon in the distance. There was a crowd of people and that's when the tragedy happened. Circus Babe had a glitch in her system that made her go psycho. She then went on a rage of manslaughter. Soon after, Funtime Fox jumps in and stops her and brings her back to the stage. Opens her hatch and fixes her. While Funtime Bear still sings on the stage. Since then the sun has never risen.

Logan Taylor (11)
Tabor Academy, Braintree

TWO SIDES OF A COIN

I wish I was in the future...
A shadow flashes in the corner. A mirror. But nothing stares back. I reached out to touch it. I will never forget that day. I was transported. Trapped. Tormented.
There were people with their eyes burned out? A scream clawed out of my throat. They turned to me, mouths foaming, and reaching, clawing and shredding at my arms. The strength of one thousand men. I sprinted, trying to get a hold of the mirror as I cried, "Please take me back! I prefer the past!"

AJ Cooper (13)
Tabor Academy, Braintree

THE WARPED SHOOTING STARS

I saw a sign with the words: *You Were Warned* written, very faded.

"What is this?"

Then it all went black. I couldn't tell whether it was the lights or I was being blindfolded.

Then, suddenly I could see that I was in a garage.

I got up as my hands and legs were free. I saw a crowbar and a hammer to my left. I grabbed the crowbar and pried the garage door open. As it opened, I saw the pitch-black sky with gleaming stars but I had a weird feeling, like I was being watched...

Hayden Stocker
Tabor Academy, Braintree

THE DRAWING COMES TRUE

The drawings predicted the future.
Alex didn't know about this yet. Until he started drawing something. It was his house and a tornado. Alex loved drawing. Something odd started happening to Alex. He felt a shiver down his spine.
His mother was watching the television in the living room. The channel changed. It turned to the weather.
The weather forecaster said, "Quickly, there is a tornado coming and it's very close."
His mum told Alex that they needed to evacuate because there was a tornado coming.
"Okay," said Alex.
He couldn't believe it. His drawings predicted the future. How?

Ellie Mouselli (12)
Wycliffe Prep School, Stonehouse

WHEN TIME IS FROZEN

Every clock had stopped. Everything was frozen except one shadowy figure who seemed to come from nowhere. The figure prowled the streets searching for the perfect victim. Slowly the figure turned and stared menacingly into the poor, helpless man's eyes. His stare was sharp as daggers tearing into the man's soul. He had found the perfect victim. The figure started ambling towards the man, stumbling with every step he took. The figure was so close now he could feel the heat of the man's breath. Suddenly, the man unfroze just as the figure had reached him but it was gone.

Liam Etheridge (12)
Wycliffe Prep School, Stonehouse

THE VIRUS TAKES CONTROL!

Ignoring the warning, I downloaded the app. A blood-curdling face popped up! My phone died!

Suddenly, an alarming voice began to announce a demand: "Give me all your personal details, or I will send a deadly virus!"

Fear went through my body! I sat there thinking. I was on my own. I felt a bulky knot tightening in my stomach, and my heart was skipping lots of beats. I was out of words. Sudden darkness came over my whole village. The lights were flickering like a demon was summoned. The whole world had lost power. What was now happening?

William Hewson (13)
Wycliffe Prep School, Stonehouse

THE CLOAK

As soon as my father put on the cloak... *bam!* He disappeared. All that remained was dust. As I picked up the cloak, I reflected back on the happy memories of our fishing holiday together. Then images of my life flashed before me. I picked up the cloak and a glass door appeared. I cautiously walked through and saw the Bounty Hunter. As I avoided him and looked outside, I saw the two moons eclipsing... A tear slowly rolled down my cheek. The cloak had shaped my life forever. I was destined to follow in my father's footsteps.

Sam Smalley (12)
Wycliffe Prep School, Stonehouse

THE NEVER-ENDING DREAM

They told me not to download it but I didn't listen. I struggled to sleep and it said it could help me.

That night, I drifted off into a deep slumber. I woke up in a forest, the roots surrounded me. I couldn't see. I slipped and stumbled over the roots until I found water. I washed my face, trying to wake myself up. But nothing worked!

My eyes opened but I wasn't at home. I was stuck in the forest. The walls seemed to close in as my heart thumped. I opened my eyes once again to find myself still not home...

Isabella Watt (13)
Wycliffe Prep School, Stonehouse

THE COUNTDOWN

Ignoring the warnings, I downloaded the app. It was a countdown to death. I had five minutes. Part of me didn't believe it was true, but by the time I clocked that I had five minutes to live, thirty seconds had gone. I started to hear footsteps. I ran up the stairs and got under the covers. I checked: three minutes left. The door creaked open. The lights flickered.
"Wake up, sunshine."
It was a dream? I grabbed my phone, and the app was already open, but it was now set at eighty years. I dread that day.

Kitty Ashbee (13)
Wycliffe Prep School, Stonehouse

DEATH IS NEAR

It all started when I was on the London Underground. I got off at Baker Street and time stopped. Nobody moved a muscle. Then all of a sudden I went around a corner and there stood a shadowy figure shaped like a human. It charged at me in a flash. It leapt, claws first at me.
Then I woke up on the London Underground. I got off the train and there were pictures of the beast in my dream everywhere. I got out of the station and there stood the very same creature as in my dream starring me down. Then it charged.

Charlie Geddes (13)
Wycliffe Prep School, Stonehouse

THE MIRROR

I didn't move, but my reflection did. What was happening? Was I going crazy? I needed to forget what happened, but my feet were glued to the floor. I had to know what was happening, so I took out my laptop and researched these strange encounters, and to my surprise, I was not the only one; I made a team. We would venture to the core. Was it impossible? I was going to help my world. Would I come back alive or in one piece? Would I ever see my father ever again? Would I save the world?

Jessica Chambers (13)
Wycliffe Prep School, Stonehouse

TRUTH OR DARE?

Ignoring the warnings from the internet, I downloaded it.
For a minute, I sat there regretting my decision. This is why
I'm the least favourite! Black, darkness, shadows; was it
mine or theirs? My brain was telling me to hide, so were my
instincts, but my ears followed the noise.
"Truth or dare? Pass it on. As ordered by the government,
you must choose one or die."
The blood was rushing through my brain like a fire on wood.
It finally got to me and I deserved it. Truth!

Isla-Sian Egan (13)
Wycliffe Prep School, Stonehouse

THE APP

Ignoring all of the warnings, I downloaded an app. Green, flashing Morse Code started to pop on my screen. I started to panic. "Mum, Mum!" I said.

Before she answered, the screen shouted, "No turning back now! Ma, waw, ma!"

I got sucked into the screen, just like a vacuum picking up a piece of food. As I was going through the dimensions of 1s and 0s, I landed flat on my back. As I opened my eyes, I saw a dark, gloomy figure waiting for me...

Jacob Ockwell (12)
Wycliffe Prep School, Stonehouse

YOUNG WRITERS INFORMATION

We hope you have enjoyed reading this book – and that you will continue to in the coming years.

If you're the parent or family member of an enthusiastic poet or story writer, do visit our website **www.youngwriters.co.uk/subscribe** and sign up to receive news, competitions, writing challenges and tips, activities and much, much more! There's lots to keep budding writers motivated!

If you would like to order further copies of this book, or any of our other titles, then please give us a call or order via your online account.

Young Writers
Remus House
Coltsfoot Drive
Peterborough
PE2 9BF
(01733) 890066
info@youngwriters.co.uk

Join in the conversation!
Tips, news, giveaways and much more!

f YoungWritersUK　　**𝕏** YoungWritersCW
◎ youngwriterscw　　**♪** youngwriterscw

SCAN TO
WATCH THE
GLITCH VIDEO!